Standing on the ancient earthen battlements, he scanned the crowd below. His eyes and other senses picked out creatures from a world more distorted even than devastated Europe. They reeked of unnatural evil; beings alien to this world and eager to taste its blood.

Sounds drifted from below. Howls and yapping, inhuman laughter and shrieks. Earl left the others and, chanting words under his breath, walked around the wall's perimeter, moving his hands in quick, decisive gestures.

Now the sounds rose in intensity. From out of the dark, roiling crowd moved a figure edged in fiery green . . .

WINTER OF MAGIC'S RETURN

Pamela F. Service

FAWCETT JUNIPER • NEW YORK

RLI: $\dfrac{\text{VL: Grades } 6 + \text{up}}{\text{IL: Grades } 7 + \text{up}}$

A Fawcett Juniper Book
Published by Ballantine Books
Copyright © 1985 by Pamela F. Service

Library of Congress Catalog Card Number: 85-7952

ISBN 0-449-70202-2

This edition published by arrangement with Atheneum Publishers

Manufactured in the United States of America

First Ballantine Books Edition: January 1987

to Alexandra Floyesta
to Floy and to Esta

contents

❈ one ❈

SUMMER THAW

WELLINGTON JONES AWOKE TO THE SOUND OF DRIPPING water. Drops fell from the eaves, then a whole patch of snow broke loose and rumbled off the roof. His eyes snapped open in excitement. They were having a June thaw!

He sat up, and the covers slid from his plump shoulders, letting a *whoosh* of cold air invade the bed. Hastily he pulled the coarse blankets around him and squinted across the small room. Of the two narrow windows set deeply into the stone wall, he looked eagerly at the one covered with real glass. The ice crystals that patterned it most of the year were gone.

If it was a real June thaw, this might be another mild summer. There had been one just four years ago when he first came to Llandoylan School, though he'd been too upset at the time to appreciate it.

Maybe Master Foxworthy was right. He'd said in geography class that in the five hundred years since the Devastation, the climate had been slowly warming again. Wellington had doubted, feeling that in his own twelve years he had seen no change worth noting. But if this

1

summer proved like that other one, there might be another August with no snow on the ground.

Slipping a hand from beneath the blankets, he fumbled along the cold stone wall for the niche where he kept his glasses. Pudgy fingers grabbed the icy metal frames and yanked them into the warmth. He scowled. He wanted to see if the icicle hanging outside his window had shortened any. But, as every morning, he didn't want to give in to these glass tyrants and put them on. They were responsible for so much of his misery.

If his eyes had been stronger (and he had been a little thinner and faster), he would be at the Cardiff Military Academy now, learning to be a warrior, as the son of a noble Glamorganshire family should be, as his parents had expected him to be when they named him for the ancient hero Wellington. Not that anyone called him that now. He was just "Welly," like the name of high boots for slogging through mud.

Angrily he jammed the glasses onto his round face and glared around the bare room. So now instead of the yearned-for academy, he was at Llandoylan School receiving a "well-rounded" education, when he wanted to be learning to fight boundary raiders from Gwent, or Angelsy pirates or perhaps the rumored hoards of muties from the south.

Of course, he'd been told often enough he was lucky to get any education at all. Children of herders or farmers generally got none.

The muffled clanging of the ten-minute bell startled him. Hurriedly he slipped out of bed, yelping as his bare feet slapped against the cold flagstones. When he was an upper classman, he'd at least have a rug in his room. He tugged on a pair of socks. Then rushing to the washbasin, he broke the ice crusting its surface and splashed his face perfunctorily with water.

Anyway, he thought as he hastily pulled on his long underwear, this was an early thaw—a time for exciting things to happen. And this time he would make the best of it.

Trousers and shirt on, he slid into his boots and, grabbing his fleece-lined jacket, rushed out the door into the narrow hallway. Still struggling with one sleeve, he rounded a corner and smashed into another hurrying body. Adjusting his skewed glasses, his heart sank. It was Nigel Williams, accompanied by several of his cronies.

"Watch yourself, Frog Eyes!" Nigel snarled. "If you don't know how to act in the presence of your future duke, I'll be glad to show you."

"Aw, later, Nigel," drawled Justin, the young lord's chief lieutenant. "The pleasure of whipping a worm like that isn't worth missing breakfast for."

Nigel snorted agreement, and without another word he and his companions turned disdainfully and descended the stairs. Welly, pale and shaking, stood on the landing until they were out of sight. Then he hurried down, slipping into the great dining hall as the final bell sounded and the ancient wooden doors closed ponderously behind him.

Hazily lit by narrow windows, the hall was noisy with premealtime chatter. Welly scanned the long tables and benches for a free place, finally sliding into an empty seat across from one of the younger students, not a friend, but at least one who hadn't made fun of him yet.

Not, he thought glumly, that he had any real friends here. Except, perhaps, Heather McKenna. But he wouldn't sit next to her here. Nigel or his sort might trot out one of their taunts: "Horseface Heather and Frog-eyed Welly, Ugly as muties and equally silly." When they did, Heather usually pointed out that the rhyme stank and that anyway frogs were extinct so how did they know what frog eyes looked like?

At last bowls of steaming porridge were being passed

down the long wooden tables. When Welly's reached him, he clamped his hands around its rough pottery sides, letting the warmth seep into them. Up and down the table, the students' breath rose in white puffs.

At the head table old Master Bigly rose and mumbled the usual invocation. "We remnant of Man thank the Creator for his mercy. As life is preserved and sustenance preserved, so hope is preserved. World without end. Amen."

Welly began eating in silence, and avoided looking at his tablemates by staring into the dim cobwebbed recesses of the vaulted ceiling. His thoughts were on how to avoid Nigel's promised punishment, though he might forget. He made too many threats in one day to keep track of them all.

Nigel had been here for less than a year and would return to the Military Academy after a stint at rounding his education. But already the big, hulking boy had made his mark at Llandoylan. Welly wondered if Nigel's boast were true, if when he became duke he'd change the title and declare himself king. Dukes of some of the larger shires had done that already. It added zest to the regular border clashes. Not that any of the shires had populations big enough for real wars. But it sounded better to fight for a king than a duke, even if Britain had a dozen of them.

After breakfast, Nigel sailed out of the hall along with the other upperclassmen, not casting Welly a glance. On the other side of the hall, however, someone was waving at him energetically. Squinting, he recognized Heather and waited while she threaded her way between the benches and departing students, light brown hair swinging in two thin braids. Her long, narrow face, though not quite pretty, was lit in an eager smile.

"Welly," she whispered conspiratorially, "I've really come across something good this time. Don't dare talk about it now, it's too big. But I'll—" She stopped and looked with exaggerated caution around the near-empty hall.

"I'll come to your room tonight. Usual signal." Then she whisked out of the room to her first class, and prickling with curiosity, Welly headed to his.

Ancient Written English was not his favorite class, but it was necessary if he wanted to read writings that had survived from pre-Devastation days. Not that Welly was anxious to read most of them, unlike Heather who read every printed word she saw. He simply reasoned that if he was too fat and blind to be a warrior, perhaps he could learn about ancient strategies and battles and be some general's clever strategist.

The morning's second class, Geography, he enjoyed more. For the last several months, they had been studying the pre-Devastation world and the nations that had flourished before nuclear war, and the cold and darkness that followed, wiped out most life on the planet.

Welly had been interested, partly because Nigel and his followers had loudly voiced their disinterest. They considered unimportant the layout of extinct nations, most of which were now poisonous, glassy plains, peopled, if at all, by sparce bands of mutants.

Master Foxworthy had stressed that the fate of all the earth was interconnected. Britain, he pointed out, had survived the worst of the war because in late pre-Devastation days it had disarmed, ridding itself of its own nuclear weapons and those that allies had placed on its soil. As a result, when war finally came, Britain was a minor target, and only the city of London, the former capital, had been bombed. Destruction from blast, firestorm and first-wave radiation had been confined to the island's now-desolate southeast.

But clouds of radiation from the bombed nations had swept the world. Debris and dust blown into the atmosphere blocked the world's sunlight, lowering temperatures and destroying most plant and animal life. The atmosphere's protective layers were thinned and harmful ultraviolet rays, plus persistant radiation, brought lingering death and terrible mutation to generations of survivors. Civilization collapsed into centures of barbarism.

Today, Foxworthy was back to the present, showing post-Devastation boundaries by jabbing a pointer into the map drawn on the skin of a large two-headed cow. The colored lines and patches showed the shires, which, sandwiched between the Scottish glaciers and the southern desert, had for centuries operated as independent duchies. For most of those centuries the boundaries had wavered as shires fought among themselves, nibbling off territory and asserting dominance.

Glamorgan's eastern enemy, Gwent, was the topic of today's class, and for once Duke-to-be Nigel paid close attention. But partway through the class, one of the older girls interrupted with a question that had been buzzing around the school for several days.

"Master Foxworthy," she said deferentially, "could you tell us whether it is true that armies of muties from the Continent have invaded the southeast and are attacking shires fringing the desert?"

"Miss Dillon," Foxworthy replied after a frowning pause, "your question, although irrelevant to the topic of today's class, none the less deserves an answer. It is true, as I have pointed out, that with the capture of water in ice and glaciers, the sea level is a good deal lower than in pre-Devastation times. Not only is our coastline farther out, but areas such as the English Channel are narrower. And they present far less formidable a barrier than once they did.

"However, the human population of continental Europe, as indeed that of most of Asia and North America, was largely destroyed in the Devastation and aftermath. Only in the non-glaciated areas of Scandanavia is there any remnant of civilization capable of organizing armies as such.

"Still, bands of mutated animals and humans do reportedly roam the continent, even as they do here on a smaller scale. And reports have been received of some having crossed into southeast Britain. But these are isolated incidents and nothing to cause concern."

Master Foxworthy glowered around the room to discourage further rumor mongering and then returned to his day's subject. Half of Welly's mind attended to the class, while the other played with strategies for smashing armies of muties on the borders of Northhamptonshire.

After classes in Math and Culture came the final class of the day, Science, which Welly and most of his classmates considered a waste of time. Perhaps the subject could be interesting, but not with Master Quiles pacing about bemoaning the loss of past glories and parroting tales of ancient wonders. And even if the grand old days and their fabulous devises had been that golden, what of it? The knowledge and skills to make those things were long gone.

But finally the intoning ended, and the students were dismissed to a supper of potato soup and barley bread. Afterwards it was still light, and many donned coats and hurried out into the walled schoolgrounds. Usually Welly would choose a game of chess or checkers, but tonight he had other plans. Heather had passed him after dinner with a theatrical wink, and he didn't want to miss her visit. Wild as her ideas usually were, they added some excitement to life.

Leaving the dining hall, he threaded his way through the familiar maze of stairways and corridors that made up Llandoylan School. The venerable building had grown steadily and with no discernable plan since an order of monks had laid its first stones over a millenium earlier. After its monastery days, it had served as a hospital, an insane asylum, a hotel and several institutes. Each new purpose had brought new additions. Nothing major, however, had been added since the Devastation, and the whole conglomerate had an aura of heavy, well-worn age.

Once Welly reached the boys' dormitory wing, he climbed the narrow back stairs to the second floor. Along his own hallway, most of the rooms were unused. Those that were not had only single occupants, following the school's independence-instilling policies. Welly, an only child, preferred this. Since most people apparently had little use for him, he had decided early not to show a need for other people. This ploy wasn't terribly effective, he realized. The others didn't care whether he needed them or not. Still, it made a defensive wall to fall back to when he was particularly snubbed.

His room greeted him with its familiar smell of cold mustiness. Gray, early evening light seeped through the windows. Through the glass one, he noted the length of his special icicle, seeing it had melted considerably during the day. Then pulling out the drawer in the old wooden table, he checked his candles. Two fresh ones and three stubs. That was all right, then. They were given only six candles per month, but since he often studied in the library, he usually had spares for needs like tonight.

Sticking a stub into the pottery candlestick, he placed his flint and steel in readiness beside it, then settled himself on the bed. In the growing darkness, he reviewed in his mind the translation he'd been reading of Caesar's campaign in Gaul. Of course, Gaul, or France, was as dead as Caesar, but the military strategies were ageless.

The room had sunk into darkness when he was startled back from Gaul by a rap at the window—one rap, a double rap, then another single. Having a code, he knew, was silly. But Heather liked melodrama. Certainly no one else would come scuttling like a spider over the roofs between the girls' and boys' wings.

Heather scrambled in along with a gust of cold air. While Welly fumbled with lighting the candle, she sat on the deep windowsill, swinging legs that, even padded in their wool-lined trousers, seemed thin and gangly. Then she hopped down, closed the window latch and perched herself cross-legged on the table.

In the flickering candlelight, her thin face glowed with excitement. Ceremoniously, she dusted off a spot on the table and plunked down the package she'd had tucked under her arm. With a flourish, she pulled aside the rag wrappings and revealed a small and very tattered paper book, obviously quite old.

"I found this in the library in the miscellaneous section," she announced proudly. "And those snippy 'social' girls say they don't need me or my bookish ways! Ha! I guess I don't need them either!" She slipped off the table and pirouetted dizzyingly around the room, braids standing out like pinwheels.

"Wait till Mable or Kathleen sees me sweeping into class bedecked with emeralds and rubies! Maybe I won't seem such a washout then!"

"Heather," Welly said, confused. "What exactly do you have there?"

"Treasure!" she declared, one hand held high like a torchbearer. "Treasure that you and I are going to find!"

Welly tried to sound cool and sauve, but his "Oh, really?" came out rather high-pitched.

"Indeed!" She slapped a hand solidly on the old volume. "In these pages, we find the true tale of Veronica Hartwell, who, back in the dim past a couple hundred years before the Devastation, was subject to dire tribulation, and in her hour of deepest despair hid her treasures away, where no man has seen them since—I hope."

"Where did she hide them?"

"Ah, that's the best part, it was right around here! It says so." She picked up the crumbling book and flipped carefully through the pages as she continued. "She was a governess, see. Sent out to wild and lonely country in Glamorganshire."

"There's a lot of wild and lonely country around here," Welly objected. "There was then too, I expect."

"Yes, but this refers to a grand old estate, Ravenscroft, nestled in wild and windswept foothills northwest of Cardiff. And then it goes on to talk about the ancient battlements where she gazed at the dismal sea."

"You can't see the sea from around here."

"Dummy, you could then. The Bristol Channel ran right up the Severn valley.'

"Yeah, that's right," he muttered. "But that description still fits a lot of territory."

"Naturally. But the best part is . . . we have a picture!" She shoved the book toward the candle, revealing a cracked and faded paper cover, showing a lovely young lady with wind-tossed hair and disheveled gown running down a path from a gloomy castlelike building. A dark caped figure pursued her, and in the background was a glimpse of cliffs and distant sea. Above it all, in barely legible scarlet letters, were the words "Desire at Ravenscroft."

"All we have to do now," Heather said triumphantly, "is find a place that fits the description and the picture, and we'll have it."

"Heather," Welly ventured after a long examination of the cover, "are you sure this isn't a work of fiction?"

She gave him a long, withering look. "I'm not that gullible. I am eleven years old and exceptionally well read. Besides," she continued as she thumbed through the old book, "I still don't believe what Master Gallowglass said about Holmes. I think he misread the historical evidence. Arthur Conan Doyle was clearly only a pen name for Dr. Watson. Anyone can tell those stories are factual accounts."

With mixed emotion, Welly recalled Heather's enthusiasm of the previous year, after she'd discovered the recorded investigations of a nineteenth-century detective named Sherlock Holmes. She had even involved him and a few of the younger children in a New Holmes Detective Agency to study the great man's methods and solve local mysteries. They'd had a splendidly exciting time until an investigation of the source of meat for the Sunday stew got them in a good deal of trouble, and Culture Master Gallowglass had disdainfully stated that the Holmes adventures were fictional stories written by an author who had also invented monsters and lost worlds.

"Anyway, this is different," she resumed. "It's clearly a historical account—readably written admittedly, but full of detail. What happens, you see, is that this young woman, beautiful, impetuous Veronica Hartwell, is from a poor but aristocratic family in Oxford. Her father, who was some sort of diplomat, dies in distant India, and she is left penniless. She's taken on as governess for the children of widower Drake Moorgrave, who lives in dark and sinister Ravenscroft Manor in Glamorganshire. Well, he has some mysterious secret in his past, though Veronica is strangely attracted to him. Then she receives a secret message from her supposedly dead father, leading her to a treasure stolen from him by Moorgrave. At last she has it in her room— lovely stuff, emeralds and rubies, and a pair of jeweled daggers—when Moorgrave, who for days had been making impassioned advances, is heard approaching. She quickly hides the treasure, except for one dagger, behind a loose brick in the fireplace."

Heather stopped dramatically. Despite himself, Welly was caught up. "Then what happened?"

"Well, unfortunately, the next part of the book is missing."

Welly groaned. "So, if this is the treasure you expect us to find, what makes you sure it's still there? Maybe this Moorgrave character found it."

"Ah." She smiled triumphantly. "It's only the middle part of the book that's missing. The last few pages are here, and they say . . . Let me get it here."

She carefully flipped over the final pages. "Here it is. 'Veronica turned again for a last look at Ravenscroft, its sinister battlements darkly silhouetted against a storm-wracked sky. She knew that she would never return there. Better to let its treasure and its painful memories remain untouched until time had cleansed them both. She would never speak of either again. Sighing, she nestled her head against Allen's (I don't know where he came in) shoulder, and the two continued down the road toward their new life.'"

"Hm," Welly said as Heather looked at him, expectantly. Then he added, "So, if this story is for real, you think we can go out, find the ruins of this Ravenscroft place, poke around in an old brick fireplace, and find necklaces and a jeweled dagger?"

"Right!"

Skepticism fought with excitement. With this early thaw, it would be fine to get out, out beyond the schoolgrounds and the town itself. And suppose they did find the treasure? That wouldn't be bad—especially the jeweled dagger.

"All right. I'm with you. When do we start?"

"Tomorrow's Sunday. If we leave early, we'll have the whole day to search."

They discussed plans until finally Heather slipped out the window again and headed back along valleys where the slate roofs came together. She could probably have used the corridors just as well. The movements of the night monitors were usually predictable. But that would have lacked excitement.

Once he fastened the latch, Welly blew out the guttering candle and hurriedly undressed. Crawling into bed, he curled up in a tight ball until his body began warming the icy coverings.

His ever drowsier thoughts dwelt on tomorrow's adventure and on his companion. Heather McKenna was his only real friend at the school. They had drifted together perhaps because they were both outcasts. She had been sent to Llandoylan, she claimed, to get rid of her when her mother remarried after the death of Heather's father. The aristocratic husband had no love for this homely girl, of Scottish refugee extraction, and her mother now needed to produce male heirs and remove visible reminders of her former lowly marriage. During three years at Llandoylan, Heather had never once been called home for holidays.

But at school she didn't find herself needed any more than at home. Her fellow schoolgirls were there primarily to become refined mates for fellow aristocrats. They felt little need for pure learning, while for Heather, learning and fantasy were what made a parched life bearable. But the more she turned to it, the more the others drove her out of their world into her own.

When Welly put aside his own reserve and joined Heather, her adventurousness chipped away at his caution. Everything he did with her ran the knife edge of trouble. She thrust an excitement into his life that he never would have added on his own.

He drifted to sleep dreaming of leading Caesar's armies with a great jeweled dagger held aloft.

In the dead of night, a sound chiseled its way into Welly's sleep. He tried withdrawing deeper into dreams, but it followed and pulled him out. Eyes closed, he lay listening, and despite the wool blankets, he shivered. He had heard that sound before.

The keening wail was faint and seemingly very distant. He'd never heard other boys mention it, but maybe no one else heard it. His was the last tenanted room in this wing. Another older section abutted this one, but its upper floors were abandoned.

The cry came again, unearthly and chillingly sad. He refused to imagine what it might be. He just wished it would stop.

Eventually it did. But still he lay awake, nerves strung as taut as bow strings. He tried to relax, but now something else kept him awake. He wished they allowed chamberpots here instead of stressing fortitude in all things. He tried to go to sleep, but was too uncomfortable. He sighed. He'd have to make a trek to the latrine.

Reluctantly he slipped from the blankets, slid his legs into icy trousers and hastily tucked in his nightshirt. Ramming his feet into boots, he pulled on a coat and stepped quietly out the door of his room. The passage was hazily lit with widely spaced candle lamps. He hurried along, listening to the flap of his boots on the flagstones and hoping he'd hear nothing else, particularly that crying. At least he was moving toward the more populated part of the building.

He descended a narrow set of stairs and took several corridors to a small back door. Outside, he hurried through the darkness toward the darker shapes of the outhouses.

On his return, he felt better and was enjoying the relative mildness of the night when suddenly he stepped into a pocket of cold air. Its chill set him shivering—with cold and something else. Then a noise came from ahead, from the front of the darkened school building.

There was the sound of crashing wood and glass, a man yelling, and a sound that could not have been a man. Welly stood rooted with fear. A dark shape hurtled toward him. It was large and low and showed the glint of eyes as it swept past. The cold in the air lapped around him like a wave, then flowed away.

The fear that held him snapped. He ran toward the building. Several voices tumbled from the headmaster's office. He wanted to learn what had happened, but they'd only send him away. And at present curiosity was not nearly as strong as a wish to be safe in his warm bed.

But once back there, sleep did not come easily. He was sure that, in the morning, there'd be some reasonable explanation for the disturbance in the school office. But if there was any explanation for what had passed him in the night, he suspected he wouldn't want to hear it.

two

BEYOND THE WALLS

NEXT MORNING, THE SCHOOL WAS ALIVE WITH STORIES ABOUT the break-in. As the students ate Sunday breakfast of porridge and stewed turnips, rumors flew up and down the tables. It seemed that in the middle of the night, Headmaster Greenhow had been disturbed by sounds from the office adjacent to his rooms. He entered and found a dark someone or something (versions differed) tearing through a cabinet of school records. Greenhow had thrown a stool at the intruder, who then leaped back through the broken window.

Several masters had answered the alarm and had immediately checked the records strewn over the floor, but none appeared to be missing. Nor was anything else gone from the room. So the motive for the break-in remained a mystery.

Welly heard no mention of any animal with the burglar and tried to conclude that he'd seen only a man in a heavy coat running low to avoid detection. That explanation did seem more reasonable than anything else, particularly after breakfast when he stepped through the school's doorway into the daylight.

It was a day to banish fears. He looked at the sky with a thrill of excitement. He'd scarcely believed it when he'd squinted through his window pane before breakfast. But it was true. The sky was blue.

Not the impossible bright blue of ancient paintings, of course. But none the less, the sky, which most days was gray or dirty white, today was definitely tinged with blue. His father said that as a boy he had never seen that. And here he, Wellington Jones, had not only experienced two June thaws but had seen several blue skies in one year. He hurried down the stone steps, glad that today was Sunday and adventure beckoned.

Heather waited not far from the main gate of the school grounds, offering crumbs to a squirrel. The fluffy black creature stuffed its cheeks as fast as crumbs were dropped in front of it. But at the sight of Welly, the animal scurried onto the high stone wall and chattered down at him.

"I'm sorry, I didn't mean to scare him," Welly said.

"Oh, that's all right. This one's Sigmund, and he's always skittish. His mate, Rapunzel, is friendlier, but she has some new babies now."

"It's wonderful how they come right up to you," Welly said admiringly. "I've never known anyone whom animals liked so much."

"Well, animals are less difficult than people. Maybe they don't exactly need you, but they're willing to let you be friends as long as you're patient enough."

Scattering the last of her crumbs at the base of the wall, she patted a bulge in the pocket of her heavy coat. "I've got a surprise for us too. I talked to Cook before breakfast. You know she really is a good soul. She gives me scraps for my friends like Sigmund here and likes me to tell her stories. Says they jolly her up. Anyway, I told her we were bound for high adventure today and would miss Sunday lunch, so she gave me some bread and even a bit of cheese. It was left from Master Greenhow's supper, but he had a headache and didn't eat it."

"I don't imagine that ruckus last night helped his headache," Welly said, then immediately regretted bringing up the subject when he saw a gleam kindle in Heather's eyes.

"Now that's a real mystery, isn't it?"

"Yes, but just let the masters and the constable deal with it. The Holmes detective agency is permanently disbanded, remember?"

He decided that, for the moment, he wouldn't even mention what he had seen in the night. He'd much rather spend the day looking for fictitious jewels than tracking down something whose memory still chilled him.

Heather laughed. "All right, one mystery at a time. Anyway, I'm more in the mood for hunting treasure than burglars who don't take anything."

She started for the gate, then stopped as a group of older students came toward it. Nigel was among them, with Melanie Witlow, his latest favorite, draped over his arm.

Seeing Welly, Heather and the squirrel, he called out, "Do be careful of the vermin, children. They might bite and turn you into muties—but it looks like they have already." The others laughed at this witticism and passed on out the gate.

"As for vermin," Heather snapped, angrily twisting the tip of a braid, "that's him. Sigmund here would make a better duke than that arrogant bully."

Welly shrugged, heading for the gate. "Well, never mind him. We've got a whole day away from his kind."

Once outside the school grounds, they walked along narrow graveled streets that wound among the varied buildings. A few were old pre-Devastation structures, while others were new, although built largely of scavenged materials.

Since this was Sunday, the streets were full of people from both town and countryside. Most were heading for one of the places of worship. There had been several in Welly's hometown, but he was always impressed with the variety here. There were Holy Catholics and several old Protestant sects, as well as Armageddonites, Druids, Israelites, and New Zoroastrians.

Most weeks he went to one or another, always avoiding the New Zoroastrians, the church Nigel's group was flirting with at the moment. But Sunday was a free day as long as students were within the school walls by curfew. Even going outside the town wall was not forbidden, though few would have wanted to.

The two adventurers soon passed through the north gate, the one rebuilt ten years earlier after a Gwent raid. Then, leaving the road, they struck north toward the hills.

Most of the ground was still frozen solid, but the thaw was softening the snow cover. Scattered around the white were darker patches where spring gray-green grass curled close to the ground like a coarse wool. There, their snow-packed boots left inverted prints, compressed white tracks on the dark earth.

The two walked in silence, enjoying the faint blue of the sky. The sun could actually be seen as a silvery disk obscured by only a thin dust layer. The air seemed mild and soon they unfastened their coats, throwing back the hoods. A breeze ruffled their hair, but except for its rustling, a vast silence lay over the world.

In low-lying spots trickles of melted snow ran together. Heather in the lead, the two hopped through a network of streamlets, their boots making satisfying squelchings whenever they missed.

Suddenly Heather halted and slapped a restraining hand on Welly's chest. "Stop! Do you see it?"

"See what?"

"Over there. It's a bird."

Welly looked in the direction of her gesture. Birds were rare sights anytime of year. He squinted, then shook his head in frustration.

"There." Heather pointed. "Over by that rock, in the pool of meltwater."

Then he saw it, a large silver-gray shape with a pointed beak and long neck. At their next step, it spread its wings, rattling its scalelike feathers, and with a scolding cry beat into the air. They watched as it circled slowly overhead then drifted out of sight toward the northern mountains.

Heather sighed contentedly. "Maybe that's what I really want to be, a naturalist."

As they continued walking, Welly asked, "Do you think there's enough today for a naturalist to study?"

"Oh, I'm certain there is. Wouldn't it be marvelous to study a bird like that? Off on your own, away from people, tracking it for weeks over wild hills until you found its den or whatever. And besides, Master Foxworthy says that with all the mutations, many creatures have never even been named. Maybe that bird could be Birdus Heatherus or something! That could give you a place in things. It wouldn't matter what people thought of you."

Welly wished she hadn't mentioned mutations. As they drew closer to the hills, he remembered stories about the muties said to roam them, both the animal and the human variety. Unsettling visions from the night before returned as well.

He cleared his throat. "Heather, how much farther do we have to go, into the hills, I mean?"

"Oh not too much, I should think. In a bit, we should be high enough for that view. Then probably we ought to head west."

Welly was getting hungry. This at least let him turn his thoughts from muties to the food in Heather's pocket.

Sunday was the one day the school served lunch, and he was glad they needn't miss it altogether. The thought of the lump of cheese was particularly enticing, and Welly forged doggedly after it up the slope.

He was puffing and panting by the time they reached a level patch. But Heather seemed undaunted. "Ah, this exercise is great! Helps work off the winter fat."

Welly sighed. He knew that exercise wasn't likely to do anything about *his* fat. He was born fat. He was convinced that, when he died, they would cut him open and find that even his bones were fat.

"Think it's about lunchtime yet?" he ventured.

"Yeah, just about. But let's check over there first. Looks like some ruins."

The level patch proved to be the bed of an ancient road. They followed it up the hill toward a cluster of ruined buildings made of the gray artificial stone popular, they'd been told, before the Devastation.

"Well, these aren't the ruins we're looking for," Heather announced. "Ravenscroft was real stone and big. But it's a good place for lunch."

Welly agreed heartily.

They sat down on a dusty slab. Fishing the cloth bag from her pocket, Heather reverently brought out a small chunk of cheese and generous slices of dark gray-brown bread.

"I wish I had a friend who was a cook," Welly said indistinctly through a mouthful of bread and cheese.

Suddenly they heard a soft thump behind them. A rustling noise prickled the hairs along Welly's spine. Slowly he turned his head.

Something hideous crouched in a broken section of wall. A mutie, the closest he'd ever seen one. Heather too was staring at it, large eyes looking even larger in her thin face.

Another mutie joined the first, and Welly thought for a minute he would be sick. They were both very short, moving with a hunched gait on bowed and twisted legs. Their skin was a mottled purple, and they had no noses, only a damp hole covered by a meager flap of skin. Though one was female, both were nearly bald, with only a fringe of white hair, which on the male carried around to a wispy beard.

It was the male (Welly had trouble thinking of it as a "man") that moved forward, growling in its throat and brandishing a lump of concrete in one hand. Both children jumped up and stepped backwards. The female mutie nimbly hopped through the opening, followed by a child. Heather found the youngster equally hideous, but its eyes were intelligent and wide with curiosity.

"I guess this spot's theirs," she whispered to Welly. "Shall we go?"

"Let's!" He raised a tremulous voice. "We're sorry to have disturbed you. We'll be going now."

Both adults growled and said something that sounded like words, but the children couldn't catch them. The muties continued their slow advance.

"The food," Heather said. "Let's leave them the rest. Maybe that'll satisfy them."

Welly didn't argue as Heather placed the remaining bread and cheese on a section of wall. "Just wanted to thank you for the use of your place," she said loudly while backing away.

After the children were several yards from the ruins, the muties scuttled over to the food. Welly and Heather turned quickly and hurried off. When Heather looked back, the young mutie was sitting on the wall stuffing bread into its mouth and watching her with liquid eyes. Tentatively she waved at it, and it waved back before somersaulting off and diving for more food.

Hearts racing, the two children trotted west over the hillside, putting distance between themselves and the ruins.

At last they slowed, and Welly said beween gasps for breath, "Don't you think we should go back now? I mean, these hills could be infested with the creatures. And it's well past noon already."

"Yes," she replied, chewing reflectively on the thin end of a braid. "But you know, this really ought to be about where the old mansion was. Let's look around a little more. If we find something, we can check it out and come back another time."

Welly grunted his assent, and they continued walking west. Dutifully he scanned the slope ahead, but his mind was on bread and cheese and the question of whether muties liked to follow such delicacies with fresh meat.

It had been interesting, he admitted, seeing muties close up like that. But they were certainly awful-looking. Still, the masters said that if mutations didn't kill or prevent reproduction they were often adaptive. Everyone whose ancestors had survived the Devastation was something of a mutant, even if only in skin color.

Darker skin kept out more harmful rays, and nearly everyone was darker than their pre-Devastation ancestors. Though, of course, there was a lot of variation. He was darker than Heather, and little Zachary Green was as dark as old leather. That older boy, Earl Bedwas, on the other hand, was very pale, like things that lived under stones.

They marched on, but Welly didn't see any grand mansions. "We really ought to turn back soon," he said.

"All right. Let's just go as far as that clump of trees."

This quickened his interest. Silhouetted against the pale sky was a cluster of rare evergreens. They approached with reverence. The trunks were twisted back, from years of battling west winds, and on their north sides the dark branches still sagged under dollops of snow. The air about them held a cool, spicy tang.

Welly was so intrigued by the trees, he failed to notice the stones. But Heather saw them.

"Look, stone walls! Oh, maybe we've found it! This could be Ravenscroft Manor."

Welly looked around to see tumbled stones snaking off through the snow. Trees grew up among the ruins, and in spots low bushes half covered the stonework. The place seemed a haven for plant life. In snow-free patches, the usual coarse groundcover gave way to richer green stuff, and colorful mosses splotched the stones.

"The setting seems right," Heather said a little doubtfully, glancing from the view before her to the bookcover in her hand. "Let's look for a fireplace."

Welly was more interested in the mosses and the odd green tendrils pushing up through the snow. Could these be ferns? He stepped over a pile of stone to examine a cluster. Suddenly his foot slipped. He grabbed at a mass of brittle twigs. A whole bush pulled free and tumbled with him into the hole.

For a moment he lay stunned, liberally covered in loose dirt. Then gingerly he stood up. Little spears of pain shot up his right ankle. Shakily he sat down upon a stone. He should have kept his eyes open! This hole wasn't exactly hidden. The ruins dropped away here, exposing a maze of sunken rooms.

Heather's thin face peered over the edge. "Are you all right, Welly? Oh, look at all you've found! I'll be right down." In an avalanche of snow and dirt, she slid down beside him. "We're bound to find something here."

"More trouble, I expect," he grumbled as he stood up again and limped experimentally about.

In an adjacent room Heather poked around in the rubble, but Welly was rapidly losing interest, even in jeweled daggers. Suddenly her voice came to him, high and excited.

"Welly, come here! Doesn't this look like a brick fireplace?"

He hobbled through the crumbling doorway and over to where a number of bricks were set into a stone wall.

"It might be," he said dubiously. "But how do we tell which is the loose brick for your secret hiding place? They're all loose."

"We'll just have to be thorough," she said, already prying bricks away and throwing them aside. Welly joined in, his interest quickened with the search.

After a few minutes, Heather stopped. "Did you hear something?"

"My stomach growling."

"No. But something was. Sounded like it came from in there." She stepped through a narrow doorway, and cautiously Welly followed.

"Look!" she exclaimed from up ahead. Hurriedly Welly pushed in beside her. The small room was still partially roofed over, but there was enough light to see a pile of branches and what looked like bones. On it crouched a small, furry animal. A pink tongue hung out of its smiling jaws, and bright yellow eyes fixed on them as the creature jumped up and made yelping bounces toward them. It was ash gray with big paws.

"How cute!" Heather said.

"It's cute all right," Welly agreed, "but we'd better leave it be."

"But how can we leave the little thing out here all alone?"

"It's probably not alone. It's sure to have family about; this looks like its den."

He glanced around the ruins with new uneasiness, imagining wild animals lurking in the cold afternoon shadows. Again he remembered the encounter of the night before and shivered. Heather picked up a bone and tossed it toward the puppy, who pounced on it playfully.

"Heather," Welly said, "let's start back now. It's awfully late."

A deep growl cut short her reply. They looked up. Glaring down at them from the wall stood a large fell-dog, ears erect, its fur gray and mottled. A limp animal dangled from its jaws. A yowling rose from behind it, and another, larger, dog joined the first. Several answering howls came from not far away.

Fear slammed against the children. Backing away, Welly expected to be leaped upon any second, but the dogs remained on the rim, yapping and snarling. Suddenly he realized these animals were afraid of them. Feral dogs had many encounters with men, usually armed men.

Quickly Welly reached down and grabbed up a brick. "Keep moving back," he whispered. "And arm yourself."

A third dog loped up and, seeing the children, crouched ready to spring. Welly lobbed his brick, and it glanced off a shoulder. The dog yiped and slunk back. The others shied away, snarling and pacing back and forth a few feet from the edge.

At the arrival of two more dogs, Heather hurled her brick. Welly followed with another and another. "We can keep throwing stuff," Heather said tensely. "But how do we do that and climb out too?"

"Maybe there's an easier way out than the one we took down." Welly reached for a stone, since they were clear of the scattered bricks.

By now, seven fell-dogs milled about, clamoring for blood yet hesitant to come for it. But larger numbers increased their confidence, and they moved closer to the edge. As the children retreated, fewer of their missiles reached the pack.

The barking and yapping were deafening, but suddenly it

stilled. An unearthly howl rose from the other side of the ruins and climbed up and up into a piercing shriek.

The dogs paced about in confusion, tails between their legs. The eerie sound came again, closer this time, and the pack slunk back out of sight. In a few moments, they were yelping some distance away.

The sound that had driven off the wild dogs rooted the children with fear. Dreading what he would see, Welly turned slowly to look in the direction of the sound. A dark shape moved to the rim of the ruins, silent against the pale sky.

"Well met, schoolmates," said a perfectly human voice. "But let's get out of here before your friends return. I can't fool them with that howl forever."

Welly just stuttered in relief, but Heather found the name of their deliverer first. "Earl Bedwas! What a rescue!"

"Here, you can get up this way," the older boy said, and he helped them up what had once been a stairway.

"Now, let's go—quickly but calmly," he said when they reached the top.

Following his lead, they moved down the slope as fast as they could. But with Welly's hurt ankle, this was not fast enough for any of them. The dogs, however, did not follow.

"I suppose it's rather obvious to say how grateful we are," Heather said to their new companion. "But thank you, just the same. How did you find us, anyway?"

The boy ran a hand through his long dark hair. "Oh, I was out walking around the hills, and I heard the pack up by the ruins. It sounded as if they had some special trouble going, so I thought I'd take a look."

"How did you do that howl?" Welly asked. "It sure scared them."

"Not just them," Heather muttered.

Earl laughed. "I don't know how I first stumbled on it. But I come out to the hills a lot, and I've gotten to know the things that live here. The fell-dogs are afraid of other dog sounds, if you do it right. Maybe they think it's the dog-devil or some such. I don't know."

The three walked single file toward the distant walled town. Welly, limping along in the rear, watched the tall, thin boy as he strode on ahead. If Earl did spend his free time wandering alone in the hills, then he was probably as odd as most people said he was. He'd never had much contact with the older boy, but whenever he had, Earl had always seemed pleasant enough. Probably he was a bit of a loner, and Welly knew that was enough to make some consider him peculiar.

When they reached the lowlands, Earl stopped and looked back at the hills. "They won't follow us here. Sit down a minute, Welly, and let me look at that ankle." Welly collapsed gratefully onto the soggy grass. Earl, kneeling in front of him, took up the injured foot and peeled back trouser, sock and boot top. Gently he prodded the ankle while Welly winced. "It's probably just twisted, though it's swelling a little. Anyway, binding will make it feel better, and you'll move faster."

He drew a linen scarf from inside his coat and wrapped it firmly around Welly's ankle. "There," he said when everything was back in place. "Want to rest more?"

Welly swallowed. "Just a bit. It hurt so much for a while, I thought I was going to be sick."

Earl nodded and sank back on the ground, his head cocked quizzically to the right. "Would it be impertinent to ask what you two were doing up there?"

Heather looked down at her hands. "We were looking for treasure."

"In the ruins?"

"Well, somewhere up there. I found a book that talked about it, and that seemed like the right sort of place. But I don't know, maybe the book really was fiction. Anyway," she concluded, looking up defiantly, "it made a ripping good adventure!"

Earl smiled, dark eyes glinting in his pale, almost gaunt face.

Welly glanced uneasily back to the hills. "Earl, are you sure the fell-dogs won't come down after us?"

The older boy shook his head. "They're afraid of people. Unless there's a famine, they don't come close to towns or roads."

"But last night . . ." Welly began, then looked quickly at Heather. "I'm sorry I didn't tell you this earlier, Heather, but I was afraid you'd want to investigate. Last night, I was coming back from the loo at the same time Master Greenhow discovered that intruder, and something big and black and low ran by me in the dark. It was cold and horrible."

Earl raised an eyebrow. "I can't even guess what it was. But no fell-dog would come that near to people unless it was rabid. And a rabid dog would have stayed and fought."

Welly lowered his eyes. "Well, maybe. I just thought that with the cries in the night . . ."

"Cries in the night?" Earl said sharply.

"Yes, that's what woke me first. High, wailing cries. I've heard them before. I just thought that maybe some animal made them, and this thing I saw could have been it."

"You're heard these cries before? Where's your room?"

At the end of the north wing, near the abandoned part. Have you heard them too?"

"No, never! It's probably just the wind or something." He stood up abruptly, tugging a shock of black hair out of his eyes. "We'd better be going, if you're feeling better."

Earl helped Welly to his feet, then smiled tautly. "From the look of the sun and your ankle, we're not likely to make it back by curfew. But if you limp impressively into Master Greenhow's study, we mightn't get too grim a punishment."

"You two could go on ahead," Welly suggested unenthusiastically. "There's no point in your getting into trouble because of my clumsiness."

"What!" Earl exclaimed. "And leave you to enjoy more adventures alone?"

"No," Heather said, her back turned resolutely on the rapidly sinking sun. "We all stick together."

✺ three ✺

FRIENDS IN NEED

EARL HAD BEEN RIGHT. THE HEADMASTER WAS IMPRESSED with Welly's ankle and the story of the others staying with him against possible perils of the night. (The actual fell-dogs and mutants were judiciously not mentioned.) As a result, the punishment for missing curfew was moderate: they were restricted to the school grounds for the next three weekends and confined to their rooms every evening after dinner.

This penalty, however, proved taxing, since the brief summer was fully upon them. For those three weeks, temperatures were above freezing every day. To miss any of such a golden time seemed terribly hard.

Heather, while refusing to lose the out-of-doors all togehter, also sought to avoid those parts of the school ground where other students might be playing or talking, activities from which she'd be pointedly excluded. Those Sundays she spent in the old orchard, a forgotten spot where the ancient school wall had been joined to the new town defenses. Most of the fruit trees that had once thrived there had long since died, but a few hardy descendants still remained. During their brief period in leaf, they were the center of much pride and some tourism.

Generally, however, the orchard remained untenanted, and Heather found it a welcome refuge. She played her own games, told stories to occasionally attentive squirrels, or sat in a corner of the wall reading.

Welly preferred to turn a contemptuous back on the weather and passed his confinement in the musty shadows of the library. Earl too spent much of his time there. The two boys had seldom spoken before, but now they explored together some of the treasures to be found among the jumbled shelves. The Llandoylan library had, in the centuries following the Devastation, become the repository for most of the surviving books in southern Wales.

Welly soon realized that Earl's interests were wider ranging than his own. In the older boy's seven years at the school, he'd been a voracious reader, gathering knowledge on a variety of subjects. Learning of Welly's interest in military tactics, Earl lead him to new sources and helped explain periods of history that had always seemed fuzzy to him. Although neither boy developed friendships easily, there grew between them a tentative openness.

One Sunday afternoon, the two were seated alone at an age-scarred table. Bookshelves towered on every side. The only light came from two high glass windows, whose filming of ancient grime gave everything a hazy cast. Dust motes danced in the slanting shafts.

After a time, Earl pushed aside his book on Italian city-states and leaned back in his chair, thin hands clasped behind his head. "Welly, I'm curious. What is it about military tactics that interests you? You don't seem the sort who likes to go out and bash people."

Welly frowned, trying to sort out his thoughts. "No, you're right, I'm probably not. If I'd gone to the Academy, I'd probably have been a flop. I don't have that leadership stuff." His voice lowered. "I'm not even sure I have the courage."

He blushed at the depth of his confession, then looked up defiantly. "But tactics are interesting on their own, you know. It's exciting to see how things work together, how you can play many steps ahead and then see it all come out."

"Yes." Earl nodded. "I think I understand. Like chess."

Welly wanted to turn the subject from himself. His old crushed hopes were still too tender. "How about you? You seem to specialize in everything."

Earl chuckled. "I read everything, about anything, and then read something else."

"Why?"

He frowned. "I don't know. It's like always being hungry. I just feel I have to learn things. Maybe there'll come a day when it all falls together and makes sense. I've been like that as long as I can remember. Ever since they brought me here, when I didn't know anything—not the language, not even who I was." He sat forward, his voice tight as he turned to his work again, "But, I guess, there's just some things one can't learn."

Welly took up his book as well, but his thoughts stayed on his companion. They'd all heard stories about Earl's mysterious background—or lack of it. How seven years ago raiders from Gwent had attempted to attack Cardiff by hauling in a wagonload of ancient exposives. The wagon toppled off a mountain road and smashed into the village of Bedwas, exploding and killing half the population.

The next day rescuers had found a boy about seven years old wandering in the ruins, babbling strange words. They sent him to Llandoylan, where the masters knew exotic languages. But all they could learn was what seemed to be his name—Earl. When he learned English, as he did quickly, it became apparent that, in the tragedy, the boy had lost all memory of his life before. So they gave him the last name of Bedwas, after his shattered village, and kept him at the school because, though destitute, he proved an apt and eager pupil

All this was common knowledge at the school. And Welly realized that though the intense, pale boy would have been considered odd in any case, his strange background set him farther apart, as did the fact that this didn't seem to bother him in the least.

Eventually the three weeks came to an end. When they'd been forbidden to leave their rooms in the evenings, the monitors had taken special pleasure in running room checks. But now that the ban was lifted, Heather wasted no time in arranging another nocturnal visit to Welly's room.

This time, when she crawled through the window, she had a battered old metal box under one arm. Into the top were punched several small holes.

"I've devoted the evenings of these weeks to an intensive training program," she announced proudly as she set the box on the table. "I brought Little John because he's a lot better at learning things than Marian or Robin, and Tuck is just hopeless."

First she took some breadcrumbs out of a pocket and sprinkled them on the table beside the box. Then she lifted the lid and tilted the box on its side. A huge purplish cockroach darted out, stood still a moment waving its feelers, then settled into eating breadcrumbs.

"Well, what do you think of him?" she asked. "I don't think you've met Little John before."

"He sure is big," Welly said, marveling at the four-inch length.

"And he's smart, too. Look at this." She fished around in her pocket and produced a small clay ball. Placing this on the table by the roach's head, she tapped him gently on the back. At first he ignored her and continued munching crumbs. Then, with an annoyed twitch of his feelers, he turned to the ball and began pushing it with his head and front legs. When he reached the edge of the table, Heather rewarded him with a fried potato slice.

"Hey, that's pretty good. Can he do anything else?"

"He can climb through hoops, but you have to put some food on the other side. And he can pull a wagon. I made a little one out of clay with a grass harness and tried to get him to pull Marian in it, but she kept scuttling off."

"Do you think he'd push the ball for me?"

"Probably. Take his chip away first."

Welly snatched away the half-eaten potato, leaving the bug furiously waggling its antennae.

"Now, put the ball down by his head. Give him a little tap—another. Right, there he goes." At the edge of the table, Welly returned the roach's prize.

Heather sat on the chair and watched her charge proudly. "I wish I could have found Marian tonight. She's a lot prettier really. More blue than purple and sort of—What's that?"

A distant sound cut the air, a thin, high wailing. Welly shivered. "Don't know. That's the sound I told you about. It comes every so often at night. I don't like it."

The sound stopped. Heather waited breathlessly and scowled at Welly when he shuffled his feet. Then they heard it again, slightly deeper but still very faint.

"Do you suppose it's ghosts?" she asked. "Ghosts of the dead monks who built this place? Or maybe banshees, wailing on the roofs of folks who'll die?"

"Hush up! I'd rather suppose its the wind or even some wild animal beyond the wall."

"Haven't you ever tried to track it down?"

"No!"

"Let's!"

"Let's not! Suppose it *is* ghosts?"

But Heather had already sprung from the chair and was easing open the door. Silently she slipped out. Welly followed reluctantly and stuck his head into the hall.

"There, it's stopped," he said quickly. "Come on back."

"No, there it is again, louder." Welly had to admit it wasn't as muffled, but that made it worse.

"It's coming from that way," Heather said, pointing left. "Bring the candle."

Welly groaned, but returned to the room. He grabbed the candle; then seeing the potato-eating roach, he steeled his nerves, scooped it up and hastily replaced it in the metal box. Candle in hand, he returned to the hall. Such an insane expedition was not quite as repellent with company—and light.

Silent as spirits, they slipped along the hall, Heather in the lead. The flickering candle in Welly's hand cast grotesque shadows over the walls. Soon they passed into the older, more delapidated part of the building. The air was musty, and the empty rooms were festooned with dust. The monk's ghost theory seemed more plausible.

Welly was about to suggest they turn back, when they heard the sound again. Closer now, it drifted down a stairwell from the floor above.

An exultant gleam in her eye, Heather hurried to the foot of the spiral stairs and began climbing. The return of Sherlock Holmes, Welly thought bitterly; but reluctantly he followed.

The corridor above seemed even more desolate. The stale air was cold, as though these higher walls were thinner. Taking the candle from Welly, Heather crouched down and examined the floor and its strewing of dust.

"It's more disturbed over here," she whispered, pointed the candle to the left. "Let's go this way."

"Do ghosts kick paths in dust?"

"Shh! Maybe banshees do."

They had taken only a few steps when the sound came again. Much louder now, it floated from around the corner. The inhuman cry bristled Welly's hair. He knew he couldn't possibly turn that corner.

But as the wailing trailed of, it was followed by soft
choking sobs. If it was a ghost, thought Welly, it was pretty
sorry about something.

They stepped around the corner and saw a closed door. It
was clean and straight on its hinges, unlike most of the rest.
The sobbing came from the other side.

Welly and Heather looked at each other, then tiptoed to
the door. Handing Welly the candle, Heather turned the
knob. The door was unlocked. She pushed, and with faint
creaking it swung open.

Something was in the room, something breathing in soft
gasps. Welly slipped in, raising the candle high. Its dancing
light showed a small room, bare except for a chair and
narrow bed. A dark shape on the bed tossed and moaned.

They stepped forward, and the light fell on a human face,
eyes closed, features twisted as though in pain.

"It's Earl!" Heather gasped.

"I didn't know he lived up here!" Welly said. "I guess
school wards get the worst rooms."

Suddenly, eyes still closed, the boy on the bed jerked and
began the strange wailing, made more chilling by seeing it
rise from a human throat.

"We've got to wake him!" Heather said. "He's having
some horrible dream."

She ran to the bedside, grabbed the boy's thin shoulders
and began shaking. With a start, Earl opened his eyes and
sat up so suddenly it nearly toppled Heather over. He looked
around wildly, snapping out strange words.

"Hold it, Earl!" Welly said. "Calm down. It's us, Welly
and Heather. Wake up!"

Slowly, the wild look faded from his face. Earl blinked
and shook his head. "One of the dreams," he said shakily.
"Sorry . . . sorry I disturbed you." He shuddered, then
began shaking uncontrollably.

Heather grabbed a blanket that had slumped to the floor

and wrapped it around his shoulders. "It's awfully cold up here."

"Yes, but I'm always like this after a dream." His teeth were chattering now. "Sorry. Can't stop it."

"Look," Welly said. "Let's get you out of here for a minute. Down to my room. At least until you warm up."

Earl looked up at him searchingly, then nodded his head. "Yes. For a minute. The dreams, they leave a . . . a feeling in the place."

Shakily he got out of bed, his bare feet white on the gray stone floor. He stepped quickly into his boots and, grabbing his jacket off the chair back, pulled it over his thin nightshirt. The three left the room and silently made their way downstairs to Welly's, checking at corners for monitors.

As they moved along, Welly wondered over this turn of events. He'd come to think of the older boy as strong and totally in control. Now they found him exiled in a cold, shabby cell and bothered with nightmares like a small child. Welly like him no less for it, but he hoped Earl wouldn't be uncomfortable at their discovery.

Once safe in the room, they bundled Earl into Welly's bed and piled blankets around him. Gradually the shivering subsided and his pale face looked less pinched and taut.

"Do you have dreams like this often?" Welly asked hesitantly.

Earl nodded. "Every few weeks. Too often, much too often."

"Tell us about them if you like," Heather offered. "If I talk about nightmares, they start seeming silly and a lot less real."

"These are always just as real." He sat up, but for a minute said nothing more. Then he began talking in a low, pained voice. "It's faces mostly. Faces and feelings. Horrible feelings. Great forces going through me and around me, and I can't stop them or control them. I should, but I don't know how.

"The faces are the worst, though. Some are beautiful, and some are not; some are very, very evil. And I know every one of them." He looked up despairingly. "But I can't . . . I can't quite remember. They have names, and I can't name them. If only I could, maybe they'd all go where they belong—and I would too. Maybe. But I never quite reach them. I can't remember!"

He shuddered, dropping his face to his hands, struggling to control himself.

Heather turned firmly practical. "These faces, do you think they're people you really knew? Before you lost your memory and came here? Your parents, maybe?"

"Maybe. I don't know. But they are real people, and I knew them. I'm sure of that. Sometimes I see things happening, things that almost make sense, but not quite. And I never have the words to describe them afterwards, even to myself."

He looked up at the two of them. "But I shouldn't trouble you with all this."

"And why not?" Heather said stubbornly. "We're friends, aren't we?"

Slowly Earl smiled, his gaunt face softening. "Yes, you are."

"Well then, maybe we can help you figure things out."

"No. Nobody can help. The dreams are with me all the time, shoved in the background maybe, but the oddest things will bring them out: a word in a lecture or a strain of music, a certain view or the way someone laughs. There're answers somewhere; there must be. If I keep looking, maybe I'll find them. But if I don't even know what I'm looking for, I can't ask you to help." He smiled and added, "Any more than you have already."

"Well, one thing we can do," Heather said resolutely, "is provide some light evening's entertainment."

She motioned him to the table and opened the roach's traveling case. Soon they were all gathered around, Earl wrapped in a blanket, watching the antics of Little John. They sent him through the ball trick several times. Then Heather produced a hoop of braided grass and coaxed the roach through it.

"Not very impressive, I admit," she said sadly. "Remember that band of traveling entertainers last year? They had real domestic dogs and trained them to do all sorts of things like jumping through hoops. But roaches just don't jump very well."

Earl fumbled in his jacket pocket and pulled out a thin wooden flute. "Let's see how he likes this. I made it several years ago when I had mice in my room. They used to come out and listen."

He settled into the chair and draped the blanket over his bony knees. Then, raising the slender wooden pipe to his lips, be began playing, head tilted to one side.

The music was thin and reedy, rising and gliding through haunting little melodies. It bubbled through the children's blood and made them want to dance. The effect on the roach was striking. At first he sat, twiddling his feelers, then slowly he began swaying back and forth, candlelight gleaming off the shining purple carapace.

"He's dancing!" Heather exclaimed. "He really likes it."

As Earl continued to play, Welly pulled open the table drawer and sorted through the clutter; bits of string and leather, interesting stones, shards of broken pottery. Pulling out a small scrap of paper, he rolled it onto a cone, crimping the edges to hold the shape.

Carefully he balanced the conical hat on the roach's flat head. Heather laughed delightedly as the insect continued its swaying dance, hat slightly askew. After a minute, the hat toppled off and fell onto the tabletop. The roach stopped his dance, wiggled his feelers, and with his front feet pulled the paper hat toward him and began to munch it.

Earl stopped playing as they all began laughing. "So much for art!" he said.

Suddenly they froze. There was a voice outside in the hall. A monitor!

In a flash, Heather scuttled out the window, Welly blew out the candle and dove into bed. Earl, too tall to hide under anything, jumped into the dark corner behind where the door would open.

There was a solid rap on the door. "What's all the noise in there?" When nobody answered, the door opened. An older boy stood in the doorwary, a candle lantern swinging in his hand. By its swinging light, Welly sat up with an imitation of drowsy, newly awakened innocence.

"Whaaa . . . ?"

"I heard voices in here. It sounded like laughter—a girl's laughter maybe."

"No, sir. It wasn't a girl, it was me, I guess."

"You? Do you often laugh in your sleep?"

"Oh, yes, sir. I mean not laughing, sort of crying— whining like. It's the dreams, you see. I have these terrible dreams sometimes. With all these faces and people doing things. They really scare me. And I'm told I cry in my sleep."

The boy grunted and stepped into the room. Crouching down with his lantern, he looked under the table and bed. He glanced behind the door where Welly hung his coat on a peg.

Then the monitor stepped back into the hall. "If you have to be a crybaby, kid, do it more quietly!" He pulled the door closed, leaving silence heavy in the room as his leather boots scuffed down the hall.

When the sound died away, Welly slipped from his bed and after several attempts lit the candle. Earl was still standing behind the door, only partially concealed in the folds of the hanging coat.

"Why didn't he see you?" Welly whispered. "He looked right at you."

"I'm thin. And if people expect to see something like a hanging coat, that's generally what they see."

"I wish I was thin," Welly said morosely. "People can expect to see anything they want; but if I'm there, they see a fat boy with thick glasses."

There was an insistent rapping at the window parchment, and its edge lifted slightly. Heather's voice blew in with a gust of cold. "If the enemy has departed, I'll take my roach and run. It's cold out here."

Welly looked quickly at the table and found that the roach had dragged the paper hat into his open tin box and was contently chewing. Welly snapped the lid down and passed the box out the window.

"Thanks for the entertaining evening," Heather said as she tucked the box under her arm and vanished into the darkness.

Welly fastened the window again and turned to Earl. The older boy had opened the door a crack and was cautiously peering down the corridor.

Closing the door again, he said. "I'll head back now. The monitor shouldn't be back this way for the rest of the night." He paused, then smiled awkwardly. "I'm sorry I wasn't honest with you the other day. But . . ."

"No. It's all right. We understand. I just hope you don't mind my using . . ."

"No, that was good thinking. Got us out of a bad spot." He put his hand on the doorknob, then turned back to Welly. "I want to thank you both for trying to help. It's good not having to handle everything alone."

When Earl had gone, Welly blew out the candle and crawled into bed. He drifted into drowsiness, hoping he wouldn't have any dreams, not like Earl's anyway. Good he'd heard about them though. He wasn't much at story-telling, not like Heather.

August that year fulfilled the promise of the early thaw. It snowed only occasionally at night, and the light powdering vanished during the long summer days. The orchard's few gnarled trees were in leaf, and an occasional bird was heard cooing and calling among the eaves. The sun stayed up late, and after classes all the students were drawn outdoors.

One evening, some of the students put together a loose ball game. Two teams were formed, and a straw-stuffed leather ball was tossed back and forth, players trying to get it over opposite goals.

Welly leaned against a wall and watched. He wanted to play. He wanted to jump and spin and catch the ball in midair. He wanted to cleverly dodge and duck around astonished opponents. But he knew better than to try.

The others jeered at him for never playing, but he knew it would be worse if he did. They'd throw a ball at him, and instead of catching it, he'd duck. He always had and always would. He was terrified that a ball would hit him in the face and break his glasses. Then he'd be blind as a bat.

Blind as a bat. He wondered, exactly what a bat was. Surely they must be extinct. But when they'd lived, had they minded being blind? Still, he believed they'd had wings, and that could make up for a lot.

He thought about wings and flying and catching a ball in midair when his reverie was broken. A scream rose from beyond the orchard wall. He recognized Heather's voice. Pushing off from his wall, he ran toward the orchard gate.

Inside, Welly skidded to a halt and stared at the scene before him. Heather crouched at the base of a tree, with Nigel standing over her. She held the body of a squirrel. It hung limply against her chest as she rocked back and forth shouting at the boy.

"Killer! Bloody murderer! You think you're so great, you can kill for fun. You're just a bloody tyrant!"

Nigel laughed, swinging his slingshot casually in his right hand. "Squirrels are vermin and ought to be killed. I'll do it if I feel like it. Same goes for human vermin when I'm duke. Remember that, Horseface!"

Welly had been standing rigid, fists clenched, eyes hazing with anger. Now a cord snapped, and he leaped at Nigel, flailing the older boy with fists, feet and knees.

Nigel recoiled, throwing an arm over his face. Then he kicked his assailant hard in the side. Welly staggered back and was socked in the jaw. He sprawled backwards in the dust.

With cries of "Fight, fight!" a crowd gathered around them. But Welly saw only his sneering enemy. He launched himself from the ground, driving his head into Nigel's stomach. They fell in a tangle of arms and legs, then Nigel was up, his fingers twisted in Welly's hair, raining blows on Welly's chest and face.

He did not pause until a hand gripped his shoulder from behind, and Earl's voice came cold and hard. "So, that's your idea of being a duke. Killing or beating anyone weaker?"

Welly was dropped like an old sack, and he scrabbled over the ground for his glasses. Nigel straightened, turning slowly to face Earl.

"No, I'll kill or beat anyone who gets in my way. Including you, misfit!"

Nigel's friend, Justin, signaled frantically to him but was ignored. So he slipped up behind Nigel and whispered, "Not him, Nigel. A year ago he—"

Nigel silenced his lieutenant with a cuff. "If this scrawny babysitter thinks he can tell me how to be a duke, he needs a little lesson!"

Huddled together on the ground, Welly and Heather

looked on in horror at what they'd brought on their friend. Earl was slightly taller, but there the advantage ended. He was thin and lanky to the point of frailty, a skeleton loosely tied together with skin. Nigel was compact and powerful. His arms, shoulders and neck were as solid as stone.

The two crouched and circled each other. The excited crowd of students shrank back to give them room. Nigel made several feints forward, but Earl didn't flinch. Then Nigel lunged to close with him, but Earl was no longer there. He'd slipped aside and now snaked out his foot, sending his opponent sprawling. Nigel bounded back up and swung a fist at Earl's jaw. Again he missed his target. His eyes narrowed to see Earl standing back, head tilted, a taunting smile on his face.

Furious, Nigel sprang, wrapping his powerful arms around the other's thin chest. Earl staggered. Then he brought up his arms sharply and broke the hold, sidestepping the hook that followed. Again Nigel jumped for him. Earl spun around behind him, grabbing his arm. In one smooth movement, he lifted Nigel off the ground and hurled him through the air. He came to earth with a jarring thump. Groggily, he struggled to sit up, then slumped back to the ground.

The fight was clearly over. The crowd dispersed, chattering among themselves. "He should have listened," one girl said to a friend. "That's what Justin was trying to tell him. A year ago, before Nigel came, that Earl did the same thing to the strongest boy in the school. Even the tough ones leave him alone now, weird as he is."

Nigel's friends had gone to his assistance, and Earl, breathing raggedly, knelt down by Welly, who was dabbing at his cut face with a sleeve.

"Let's get out of sight," Earl advised. "He won't want a return match for a while, but the less we rub it in, the better."

Heather nodded, looking sadly down at the squirrel. "Let's take Sigmund away and bury him. Nigel wanted the pelt. But he shan't have it!"

She gathered up the lifeless body, and the three children walked quickly toward the far end of the orchard, out of sight of the others.

As they walked along, Welly said, "That was incredible fighting; where did you learn it?" As soon as he said them, he regretted the words, but Earl didn't seem to mind.

"I don't know. I've fought like that for as long as I can remember. Most of it's being quick and light. The ones who most pride themselves on their fighting are usually as agile as oxen."

Heather stopped by a stump near the orchard's far wall. "Let's bury him here. Kids never come this far. But Sigmund's family does."

She placed the squirrel on the stump, and Welly found a sharp-edged rock and started digging. The ground was hard, and after a while he stopped. One eye was beginning to swell, and he was having trouble seeing, though his glasses, at least, had been found intact. Earl took over digging.

Heather left them to gather a bouquet of leaves. She would have preferred flowers, like they used in the books, but there were few flowering plants even in summer. When the hole was deep enough, she lowered the squirrel into it. Tears streamed silently down her cheeks as Earl filled in the dirt and she strewed leaves over the little mound.

Smearing tears away with dirty hands, she said, "I know it's silly to make such a fuss over a dead squirrel. But they . . . they made a place for me in their lives. Oh, I know it's not the same as really being needed, but it was somewhere I fit in."

"You fit in with us," Earl said, putting a hand awkwardly on her slumped shoulder. "Come on, let's rest against the wall. There's a bit of sun."

They sat at the base of the old stone wall, its rough surface faintly warm. Peace seemed to seep from the patient stones and the cool evening air.

"You know," Welly said after a while. "That's the second time you've gotten us out of a bad spot, Earl. We're really in your debt."

"Nonsense."

"Oh, but we are," Heather insisted. "If it wasn't for you, we'd either have been eaten by fell-dogs or pounded into footstools for Nigel Williams. We ought to swear you eternal fealty or something. Be your bound knights, as in days of old!"

A look of conviction on his battered face, Welly stood up. "And so we shall! We'll kneel at your feet and offer you our swords!"

"Except we haven't got any swords," Heather pointed out.

"Well, we'll find some!" Welly insisted. Heather jumped up to join him, grief submerged in new purpose.

The two scurried off to find something suitable, while Earl watched. He supposed this was silly, but it was something they needed, all of them. And it had a rightness that seemed, somehow, to stretch beyond the moment.

The others returned with two short sticks and dropped to their knees in front of the older boy, presenting the sticks to him. Lowering his voice, Welly intoned, "We hereby offer you, Earl Bedwas, our swords and our eternal fealty."

Earl closed his eyes. A feeling of odd recollection swept over him and was gone. He tried to think what he should do next. Then taking their swords, he tapped the points on each of their shoulders and, with a flourish, handed their weapons back to them. "Rise, Sir Welly, Lady Heather!"

Heather jumped to her feet, braids bouncing and cheeks glowing with excitement. She leaped to the top of the stump, raising her stick into the air. "From now on, we'll follow wherever you lead and loyally do your bidding. The doers of evil shall be vanquished. Your quests are our quests, your enemies are our enemies!"

Earl looked ruefully toward the orchard gate where Nigel and his friends had disappeared. "That last, anyway, seems likely to be true."

four

SHADOWS IN THE STORM

THE TIME OF COLD WEATHER HAD COME AGAIN. THE LEAVES on the orchard's few trees turned brown and fell to the ground. And the ground itself was often covered in snow. White feathers and ferns of ice grew on glass-paned windows, while wind from the north carried the raw bite of Scottish glaciers.

The friendship between Welly, Heather and Earl grew slowly and gently. Despite his accepting their friendship, the other two knew Earl was still a loner. They respected his need to be alone. But when he occasionally sought out their company or offered to help them with schoolwork, they were pleased.

They worried about him, too. Now that they knew him, they noticed there were times when he was clearly troubled. Some mornings he came to breakfast his pale face more ashen than before and dark shadows rimming his eyes. They guessed he had dreamed again.

But Welly heard no more cries in the night. He suspected

Earl, trying not to disturb them, had muffled the door with one of his too-few blankets. But he was a very private person, and his friends would not mention it first.

During the icy weather, Heather made few nighttime excursions to Welly's room. But one night in November, she ventured again over the roofs. She was bursting with ideas, and Cook had given her a rare honeycake, which, after due consideration, she decided to share with Welly.

The two sat on chair and table in the candlelit room, savoring every sweet crumb. When at last there was no more to lick off finger or lip, Heather sighed and tucked her legs under her.

"You know, there really ought to be some way we can help Earl."

"What do you mean?"

"Well, here we are, his sworn retainers. He's obviously troubled, and we aren't doing a thing about it."

"But what can we do? The troubles are inside him. They have been for years. If it helps him to talk about it, he knows we'll listen. But if he doesn't want to, we can't make him."

Heather tugged absently on a braid. "No, but the root of the thing is that he doesn't know who he is. If we could help him learn that, we'd be doing a lot."

"But how can we find that out, when he hasn't a clue himself?"

"Oh, but there are clues. They just need tracking down. Take that language he was speaking when they found him. There's a fine clue."

"Sure, but the masters didn't know it, and he stopped speaking it after he learned English. Now he says he doesn't remember it at all."

"I'll bet that's what he was speaking when we woke him during the dream."

"A lot of good that does if he can't speak it when he's awake."

"Well," she persisted, "the very fact that he was speaking a weird language when they found him suggests that he or his family didn't originally come from that village, doesn't it? And if it was strange to the masters here, it's probably not a Yorkshire dialect or anything like that, but something really foreign."

"Such as?"

"Well, I don't know. Most foreign places aren't supposed to exist anymore. But there is Scandinavia. Maybe he comes from there."

She chewed thoughtfully on a braid, suddenly almost chomping it off. "Suppose . . . suppose Earl isn't his name at all! Suppose it's a title! Maybe he's the earl of someplace, someplace in Scandinavia. And somehow he got lost over here and was hit on the head during the explosions."

"Well, I suppose it could be, but how would we prove it?"

"Maybe just suggesting it would bring it all back."

Welly only grunted.

"Or maybe it isn't Scandinavian," she ventured, "but Russian."

"Russian? All the Russians died during the Devastation."

"Surely they *all* didn't. I'll bet there were some Russian diplomats over here . . . or spies. And when war broke out, they went into hiding. They were afraid to tell anyone they were Russians. And their descendants didn't tell either, but secretly they kept up the old ways and spoke Russian at home. And then came the explosion at Bedwas, and Earl is the only one left."

"I like the Scandinavian earl better."

"So do I. But being the secret descendant of Russian spies would be exciting."

She resumed chewing her braid, finally sighing and

untucking her feet. "But you're right. There's not much we can do unless he wants us to. He's too good a friend to intrude on."

Earl himself was indeed troubled. Increasingly so. The dreams were coming with greater frequency and strength. Sometimes he was so gripped in horror, he was unable to make a sound. When he finally awoke, he was exhausted and afraid to sleep for the rest of the night.

Increasingly, too, strange feelings held him during the day. His schoolwork suffered, and often his mind drifted off during class. His teachers noticed, but had said nothing. For that he was grateful. He was afraid they'd decide he was going crazy. In fact, he almost wished he was. It seemed the less complicated solution. But less complicated than what, he wasn't sure.

By the end of November, the tension was becoming unbearable. Whenever possible, he avoided people, including his two new friends. But when he was alone, he was intensely restless.

One Sunday morning, he awoke with a feeling of enormous pressure, pressure from inside. He felt he'd explode if he didn't do something. There was an acrid taste in his mind, a remnant of the night's dream. Bitter, distorted feelings lingered like smoke in the corners of the room. He had to get away.

Hurriedly he dressed in outdoor wear. Slipping downstairs, he left the school grounds as soon as the gates were opened, not bothering with breakfast. Aimlessly he wandered about the winding streets, hoping to find some relief. Early worship services were beginning, and from various buildings came chants, singing or ritual music. Standing irresolutely before the Armageddonite temple, Earl glanced up beyond the town wall, and his eyes fell on the dark smear of the hills beyond. Something inside him settled. He headed down the street toward the north gate.

Once outside the walls he felt better, no less tense but purposeful. He began walking northeast into the hills.

The snow on the ground was deep, and moving was more like wading than walking. As the morning progressed, the sky thickened. Slowly great white flakes sifted from it. Feathery soft, they fell silently around him. Looking up, he watched them spiraling down from the sky until he grew dizzy. Then he trudged on.

He had no idea where he was going, but he had to go. Stopping for a moment, he experimented. Turning to the west, he deliberately set off in a new direction. Within a few steps, the tension and unease returned. They grew until he could barely force himself on. When he turned back and headed northeast again, the anxiety ebbed away. He shrugged and moved northeast. There seemed little to lose.

He walked for hours. All the while the snow came more and more thickly. At first it fell in windless silence. But eventually a wind rose, blowing the snow in long streamers past his face. That wind howled with a voice of its own, and almost it seemed he could understand it.

Suddenly a new feeling came over him. He slowed. Nothing looked different. In the blowing whiteness, the sky blended with the earth. Yet there seemed to be a darkness just beyond the white. A waiting darkness, and it was evil.

Very slowly, he advanced. The wind howled more fiercely, but he sensed a new sound just beyond hearing. Further on, he heard it, separate now from the wind. Strange, unearthly sounds, voices and yet not voices.

A speck of light appeared in that darkness, the darkness he felt and couldn't see. And the light was real. Impossible, a fire burned in the snow ahead. And the voices, for voices they now seemed, came from around it.

He halted. There were shapes moving about the fire, dark and wildly leaping shapes. He crept closer. The fire rose, a tall unquenchable pillar, and around it figures jerked and danced. Some were human, others something else. The voices sang and chanted in a strange language or in no human language at all. Yet the words played on the edge of his mind, almost tumbling into meaning.

Closer now, he picked out one figure among the others: a woman, tall and slender, pale as snow. Her black hair and robes billowed wildly about her. Arms upstretched, she uttered a howling chant. Then she looked down into the fire, and he saw her face.

He screamed! He knew that face. Instantly she looked up. Her green eyes stared directly at him, piercing the glare of the fire between them. Jabbing a long white hand into the storm, she shouted, a word full of terrible power. The word went on and on, and endless stream of hate.

Around him the world seemed to shatter, and the bonds that had drawn him cracked. Turning, he ran.

The sound followed him, jabbing at his mind. He must get away from it and from that face. They must not get him!

The horrible sound faded at last, but he knew they were following. He floundered on, every step weighed into painful slowness. Snow clung to his body and blinded his eyes. Was it an enemy, too?

No, it was indifferent, didn't care. But he could use it. He could hide in the storm. They might not see, they might not find him.

He willed himself unseen. To be one with the snow, part of the storm. Snow swirled into his mind, filled his body with cold. He became the cold, the sharp biting wind. He had no breath but the wind, gusting in and out. He had no head, no legs. Only thin white windblown snow. There was no up, no down, only directionless swirling. Swirling around and forward, always forward.

On and on he went, while a small corner of his mind screamed in fear. He was the snow. Or he was mad. But surely he was dying. No breath, only the wind. He was dying in the storm, as the storm.

He must gain control, fix on someting solid, something real. Vaguely his mind saw the stone archway of the school gate. He concentrated on it with all his power. Stone by stone, he built the picture. Every irregular, hard gray shape: he could feel their roughness, the soft crumbling mortar between them. They were hard and real and fixed to earth.

In the morning, they found him sprawled in a drift, outside the school gate. His fingers were thrust into a crack between the stones.

⧉ five ⧉

THINGS OF NIGHTMARE

FOR TWO DAYS, EARL HOVERED BETWEEN LIFE AND DEATH.
They wrapped him in blankets and laid him in a bed by the
fire in Master Greenhow's study. A doctor was summoned,
but could say only that the boy was suffering from extreme
exposure. Keep him warm, he advised, but only time would
tell if he lived or died.

Gradually, however, his breathing became stronger and
faint color returned to his cheeks. The thin hands lying pale
against the blankets were no longer clammy and cold.

He regained consciousness, but despite questioning, had
little to say. It seemed he had gone out into the hills, as he
often did, and become lost in the blizzard. It was a miracle
he'd found his way back at all.

But the recovery was not even. He soon fell into a fever,
and for several days floated in and out of delirium.
Whenever they could, Heather and Welly visited him; but
he was always either sleeping fitfully or wracked with fever,
tossing about and babbling strange words.

On the fifth day, the fever broke. When his friends came, they found him propped up in bed, gazing into the low bank of flames that flickered in the stone fireplace. He turned his head when he heard them and smiled wanly. "They say you've come every day."

"We have," Heather said as they hurried to him. "And it's about time we found you looking better. You've had us worried, you know."

Welly pulled up a chair for himself, and Heather sat down on the foot of the bed. For a while they said nothing. The firelight played warmly over their faces and the backs of books on the headmaster's shelves.

Twisting her braid, Heather said, "Earl, the masters are using you as an object lesson against doing stupid things. But you have too good a head on your shoulders to just go out and get lost in a storm. What really happened?"

Earl coughed and nodded weakly. "I wish that had been what happened." He looked at the two of them a moment, then back to the fire. "I can tell you, though, as much as I understand.

"I went out because something compelled me. I don't know if it was from inside or outside. But something was going to happen, something that touched on me, on what I am. And I had to be there."

"Did you find it?" Welly asked.

Again Earl nodded. "It was something very bad. Evil. There were things there I almost knew, almost understood. But I've lost the key."

"What was there?" persisted Heather.

"I wouldn't soil words with it, even if I could. But there was someone I knew, a face. The name was just out of reach, but the face I knew."

Heather leaned forward. "A face from the dreams?"

"One of them. A woman, beautiful, and very, very evil. Once I knew that, I ran. They followed. They were after me, but . . ." A look of pained remembrance clouded his face. "But I escaped."

"Well, that's good then. You got away." Welly said cheerfully.

Earl's reply was very quiet. "It would be better if I knew *how* I got away."

Heather patted his hand. "That's no matter. You're a skilled outdoorsman, and you made it back. That's all that counts. The doctor says that if you rest and drink that nasty broth Cook makes, you'll be up in a week or two."

"He also said," added Welly, imitating the nasal falsetto of the town's doctor, "No more traipsing about in storms for that young man. I certainly hope he's learned his lesson."

Earl laughed ruefully. "I didn't learn what I needed. But I'll do my best about the storms."

As weeks passed, Earl recovered steadily. His mind too was more at ease. He would gladly have dismissed the whole thing as a particularly dreadful dream if the images hadn't stayed so vivid. He was oppressed too with a curious sense of waiting, of suspension between two acts of a drama.

Meanwhile, the year progressed, and Yule was drawing near. This was one celebration all post-Devastation religions shared. It marked the Turn of Seasons, or the Savior's Birth, or Hanukkah, or the Victory of Light. It was celebrated on the winter solstice, December twenty-second.

Earl was now fully recovered, but stayed close to home, in the library or his room. The first day he ventured from the school grounds was the Sunday before Yule, when he decided to go into town and buy gifts for his two friends.

Every year, the headmaster gave each student a few coins as a Yule gift. Earl had saved most of his, never finding much he thought worth buying. But having two friends in his life seemed to call for something special. So this Sunday he scooped his little sack of coins into his pocket and set off into town.

He had no clear idea what he wanted, but he figured he'd know when he saw it. Shops were open and temporary stalls set up to accommodate pre-Yule shoppers. Some merchants and customers had come from miles away, and the snow in the streets was churned to dirty slush. Candles burned gaily in windows, colored awnings fluttered, and everywhere people seemed happy and busy.

Earl looked at the candlemaker's stall, the leather shop and places where they sold woven goods of wool and flax. He wished he could buy Heather some fine fabric. She was, he believed, much less homely than she thought, and maybe a splendid new dress would help her agree. But he didn't have enough coins for anything but undyed browns.

Today the festivities were aided by a traveling fiddler. For a time Earl stood amid the jostling crowd, eyes closed, listening as the strains soared between carefree dances and melancholy laments. A snatch of tune brushed lightly at a memory but was gone before he could catch it.

He pushed the occurrence aside and continued examining shops and stalls. The woodcarver's appealed for its tangy smell and the feel of its wares. But wood was rare and expensive, as was the glass blower's beautiful work. Both the potters and weavers of grass made things that were useful but of little beauty.

For a while he was drawn to the hot orange glow of the blacksmith's forge, to the heavy musical clanging of the hammers and the sheer strength of the man who wielded them. Of course, Welly would love a sword, but for tht he'd need a true liege lord or at least a friend who was a good deal wealthier.

He joined a ragged cluster of children hovering about a booth selling special Yule foods. The spicy odors were painfully enticing, but friendship, he felt, deserved something more enduring.

He was becoming discouraged when, wandering down a

side street, he came upon an ancient half-timbered building housing a small antiquities shop. His spirits lifted. Surely he would find something special here.

As he opened the narrow door, setting the bells jangling, a little bald man bustled out of a back room. Wrinkled and bent over, he seemed as ancient as his wares. The man noticed Earl's student garb, which in most cases marked one as an aristocrat, and he became properly differential.

"May I help you, young sir?"

"Perhaps, but I want to look around first."

"Certainly, certainly, I am at your service." And he began pottering around a relic-strewn table in the back.

The cluttered shop smelled of intriguing, musty age. Earl's eyes wandered over the shelves, tables, cases and boxes that lay on all sides and overflowed with a profusion of interesting items. On one shelf stood a stack of shiny rectangular trays with raised inside divisions. They were made of the soft ancient metal, aluminum. But though attractive, they didn't seem of much use.

There were shelves of antique pottery much finer than anything produced today. And there were even cups of the rare substance, Styrofoam. He knew his funds weren't equal to those.

What delighted him most were the items made from plastic. The ancient material was so smooth and light, and he wondered over the lost process for making it. Perhaps he had enough money for a small item of plastic.

Old fabrics hung in the back of the shop. Some were lovely, with an exotic feel, probably artificial materials like woven plastic. Even where faded, the rare colors spoke of ancient wealth and gaity. But most were mere worn tatters, and all seemed too frail for the modern world.

In one case, in a far corner, were piled trays of jewelry. He had to shove aside decayed shoes and a stack of grooved black disks to see into it.

While ostensibly doing repairs at his back table, the old proprietor watched him keenly. Earl cleared his throat, trying to sound as though he examined expensive antiques every day. "Could I look at that tray, please."

"Certainly, sir, right away." The man scurried over and pulled out the tray. He hovered like a spider as the boy ran thin fingers through the small glittering treasures. Earl knew that many were beyond his price, but some were not. Perhaps something here for Heather. Wearing some of these could make anyone feel beautiful.

He picked out and replaced several pieces, and then took up a small gold ring. It wasn't real gold, but some gold-looking metal. It had a broad band with spiral patterns around the outside. Set into it was a purple jewel, glass not amethyst, but it was nicely cut and sparkled in the light. He turned it over in his hand and saw writing on the inside. Holding it up to a dust-filmed window, he made out the words, "Cracker Jack."

He wondered what that meant. Some ancient charm or good luck phrase? He didn't know, but the thing felt right. It seemed bright and cheery, like Heather herself.

"I'll take this," he said firmly. "And I'll need something else." He looked into the case again, squatting down to see the lower shelf. Many small objects were jammed together, including parts of several chess sets. "I'd like to see some of those." He pointed, and the old man bobbed his head and brought out a handful of chessmen, spilling them carefully over the case top.

Some were wood, one was made of stone, and several were metal. But the ones that caught his eye were of plastic. He picked up a black bishop, admiring its cool feel, it smooth surface. Then he put it down in favor of a knight, its plastic the creamy white of fabled ivory. The figure was a horse head, but not a modern horse, heavy-browed and shaggy. This horse had a high, arched neck and delicate face. A proud mane bristled along the neck from its base to the small pointed ears. He would get this for Welly, a token of his friend's knighthood.

At last Earl left the shop, carefully clutching the gifts, which the proprietor had wrapped in a scrap of wool. He was so pleased with his purchases he wanted to open the package and look at them again, but decided against it for fear of dropping them in the slush.

This visit had almost finished his savings. Back at the town square he pulled the coin bag from his pocket and stuffed the small parcels inside. Then glanced up to find Heather looking at a booth, just across the street.

Jumping guiltily, he crammed the bag deep into a coat pocket as Heather turned and waved at him. "Oh, Earl," she said running over to him, "isn't the town exciting just before Yule? Everything's so bright and happy, and everyone's got their decorations up. You've been window shopping, too?"

"Yes, I have." His voice sounded uncommonly high to his own ears.

"I've been at it all morning," she said dreamily. "But if we don't want to miss lunch, we'd better hurry back. Cook said there might be something special, Sunday lunch before Yule, you know."

Together they walked up the street toward the school. As they walked, Earl began to feel odd: strangely chilled and out of focus. He wondered if he was ill again. Perhaps he'd eaten something bad at breakfast?

Heather was talking, but he found it hard to concentrate on her words. Then something she said riveted his attention. "Did you see that woman watching us? She's so beautiful. I'd love to look like her."

He stood still, started to turn then stopped. "Describe her to me," he whispered.

"Well, her skin's pale—like yours really. And she's got lovely long black hair, all tumbling out of her hood."

"And green eyes," he said flatly.

"I can't tell, she's too far. But she certainly seems interested in us. Do you know her?"

"She's the woman in the storm, in the dreams. I must get away, mustn't let her know I've seen her."

They started walking up the street again, Earl trying to hide his tension. "We can lose her in these alleys," Heather suggested. "If that's what you want."

"Yes, let's try."

They reached a corner. The buildings sagged comfortably toward each other across a narrow alley. With seeming nonchalance, they turned right. As soon as they were out of sight, they broke into a run, slipping and sliding over the half-frozen slush. Abruptly they skidded into another alley and, farther on, into another.

At last the maze opened between two buildings not far from the school gate. Looking cautiously in all directions, they saw no cloaked figure and pelted across the last open space and through the gate.

Once inside the school, Heather leaned against a pillar and panted for breath. She'd found the escape great fun and was about to say so, but a glance at Earl's ashen face showed he'd considered it anything but fun.

"Thank you," he said shakily. "I'm glad you were there. Better get to lunch now."

They parted, and Heather was not greatly surprised when Earl did not come to lunch. It was a pity, she thought, because they had meat. Not little bits in stew, but great steaming slices of it on bread. She ate with Welly, and in a hushed voice told him about the adventures of the morning.

For two days, nothing happened. They saw Earl only in class, and there he seemed tense and distracted. Dark circles had reappeared under his eyes.

On the afternoon of the third day, they were in Culture class, the only period all three shared. The subject for the day was ancient architecture, and the master was extolling structural steel. Halfway through, the class was interrupted by the entrance of a monitor. He went to the master, muttered something, then walked down the benches directly to Earl.

"Master Greenhow wants to see you in his office. He has some strangers with him."

Color drained from Earl's face, and for a moment he looked as though he would faint. Then, woodenly, he stood up and left the room. Welly and Heather exchanged worried glances.

With leaden steps, Earl walked down the corridors. The ancient stone walls pressed in heavily around him. He was walking into a trap; he knew it. But like a helpless animal, he couldn't understand or prevent it. At the office door, he forced a hand up and knocked.

"Come in," Master Greenhow's voice said through the heavy oak door. Mechanically Earl obeyed.

"Ah, Earl, have a seat." The master waved at a straighbacked wooden chair beside his desk. Earl sat and raised his eyes. Across the desk, seated in chairs by the records cabinet, were a woman and a man. The woman he knew and tried desperately not to show it.

"Earl, let me introduce you to two relatives of yours. Your Aunt Maureen and Uncle . . . Garth, was it?"

The man nodded. "Uncle Garth," he repeated in a gravelly voice.

Earl turned guarded eyes on the man. He was large and powerful looking. His skin was darker than his companion's, and under a thatch of coarse gray hair, his eyes were pale and close-set. He smiled broadly at Earl, showing yellowed teeth.

"Little Earl," the woman said musically, "can it possible be you? I hardly recognize you, you're so . . . changed. But of course you would be, wouldn't you? The magic of time and all." She laughed gaily.

"You really are a very fortunate boy, Earl," Master Greenhow said. "Your aunt and uncle have been looking for you a long time. They tell me your parents were merchants and that you grew up in Denmark. Then, it seems, you and your parents came here to Wales to tie in with the wool trade, and were never heard from again."

"Yes," the woman continued, "my dear sister and her husband and child. Garth and I searched for them every time we were in this country. Then recently, by sheer chance, we heard of the accident at Bedwas and the poor little boy they found wandering about."

She sat forward, her green eyes studying Earl very closely. "Is it true then, Earl dear, that you've completely lost your memory? You remember nothing that happened to you before you were . . . seven?"

"That's correct. I remember nothing." He clipped off his words, hating even to talk with her.

"Yes. Yes, I can see that you don't." She sat back, relaxed again. "Dear boy, how very good it is to have finally found you."

She turned to her companion. "You know Garth, he really does look the same, now that we now who he is. The same intelligent little face, the same mannerisms, the same tilt of the head."

Instantly Earl straightened himself.

"Well, Madam," Master Greenhow said, "it certainly is wonderful to find where Earl belongs and have that mystery cleared up. So that language was Danish. Well, well!" He chuckled. "I barely knew there were any Danes left to speak it."

The headmaster leaned back in his chair. "Of course, we'll miss Earl, though I understand your wanting to take him with you. He's a bright boy, and he's been a good student. He would need to be, you know, for us to have kept him at Llandoylan. We are a quality school and don't usually take charity pupils."

"Oh, but this won't be charity now," Aunt Maureen said silkily. "We're not exactly wealthy, but we've done quite well in the import business. We can leave you a little now and send you more later, to help make up for your years of kindness to our dear boy." She smiled sweetly at him, and Earl felt his insides knot.

"Well, that's very generous of you!" Greenhow bubbled. "Very generous. Now, will you be wanting to take him with you this afternoon?"

Maureen started to reply, but Earl interrupted. "I can't go this afternoon. I have to pack and . . . and say good-bye to friends."

"Oh, certainly," the woman said soothingly. "We understand, dear. This all must be quite a shock to you, and with you recently so sick. Master Greenhow tells us you were delirious for days after being lost in a blizzard. What a dreadful experience."

Earl lowered his eyes. "Yes, Ma'am. But I'm better now. I just remember that I was sick."

She smiled. "Poor thing. A bad sickness can be so confusing. And now on top of it we add this big change. One moment you're a mysterious orphan and the next you have a past—and a family. Of course, we can wait, dear. We'll stay the night in town and be back for you in the morning."

After parting cordialities, the woman swept out of the room, followed by Uncle Garth, who gave Earl a loving grin that set his spine tingling. The boy looked after the two numbly, scarcely hearing Headmaster Greenhow's words of congratulations.

That evening, Welly and Heather were alarmed at their friend's absence from dinner. As soon as the meal was over, they hurried up to his room and found him stuffing his few possessions into a backpack.

"What's all this?" Heather said breathlessly. "There's a

rumor going about that you've found some long-lost relatives. Are you really leaving?''

"Yes," he said coldly. "I'm leaving, but not with them."

Welly plumped himself down on the room's one chair. "What do you mean?"

"Those people aren't relatives, or if they are, I'd as soon they stayed lost. True, I know nothing about my past. But what they said was all wrong. And those two were the most wrong of all."

Earl tied up his pack and leaned back against the wall at the head of his bed. "She was very anxious to confirm that I remember nothing about my life before coming here. And I don't! But I do know that whoever she is, she is loathsome and bears absolutely no love for me."

"But still," Welly said practically, "couldn't you use them to find out something more about yourself?"

"Yes, I probably could. That woman holds some of the keys I'm looking for. But I'll find out who I am some other way, or I'll just get along without knowing."

Heather sat down on the edge of the bed, chewing her braid. "So, you're not going with them in the morning, then?"

"I'm leaving tonight as soon as the building's asleep, and going as far and as fast as I can before morning."

"But where will you go?" she asked.

He looked down at his pack forlornly. "I don't know."

Welly stood resolutely "Well, you can't just go barging off into nowhere, and you certainly can't go alone."

"Right!" Heather agreed.

Welly continued. "The best thing would be for you to find someplace nearby to hole up until things blow over. Heather and I can slip out at night and bring you food and let you know how things stand here. Then when the coast is clear, we'll ferry you off someplace planned."

"He could go to my family's place," Heather said

gloomily, "but they'd probably turn him back . . . or sell him."

"Yes." Welly frowned. "In any case, this will give us time to organize something, so he doesn't end up working in the mines or snatched by slavers."

For the first time in days, Earl smiled. "It certainly is good to have a strategist for a friend. I admit I hadn't given much thought to anything beyond getting away. But your slipping out to bring me food sounds too dangerous."

"Nonsense!" Heather said, jumping up from the bed. "We're your pledged retainers, remember? Besides, when have we ever turned our backs on adventure?"

After leaving Earl's room, Heather slipped down to the kitchen to persuade Cook to send him up a meal. It was strictly against the rules. But Cook had heard rumors of the boy's good fortune and was anxious to be part of the excitement and see the reportedly beautiful aunt when she returned next morning.

"No, it wouldn't be kind," the stout woman agree, "to send that poor quiet boy off without so much as a scrap of bread for his last dinner with us, and him having been so sick and all. You just take this dinner up to him and bring the dishes back when there aren't too many masters watching."

Hurrying upstairs with the food, Heather felt guilty about deceiving Cook. But maybe once Earl had escaped, they could let her in on the intrigue. Maybe she'd even help smuggle out food.

Later in their separate rooms the three waited tensely for the agreed two hours after bed curfew. Then Heather stole silently over the roof to Welly's room, and the two met Earl in his.

The three figures, dressed in fleece-lined trousers and hooded coats, crept quietly through corridors and stairways toward the small back door. They reached it, having caught no glimpse of a monitor, and breathed a collective sigh of relief.

Confidently Welly lifted the ancient iron latch. Frost furred the inside of the door hinges, but they opened with barely a protest as the oak doors swung outward. Welly jumped onto the top step and looked directly into the swinging lantern of a monitor returning from the outhouse.

The upperclassman grinned maliciously at the three startled faces. "Well, well," Nigel sneered. "I suppose you are all geared up like that, backpack and all, just to go to the loo?"

"We might be" Heather said, chin stuck forward.

"But you're not, are you? First our precious little foundling discovers some new relatives, then he and the other rejects are slipping off somewhere in the dead of the night. I want to know why and where."

"It's quite simple, Nigel," Earl said stepping down into the snow beside him. "I'm going away. And if I choose to leave this school tonight instead of tomorrow morning, that's my business. Either way, we're out of each other's lives."

"It's not quite that simple, is it?" Nigel put the lantern down on the steps and crossed his arms. "Everyone knows that aunt and uncle of yours promised Greenhow a bundle of money for feeding your miserable carcass all these years. So whether you want to go with them is irrelevant, isn't it, since they're not likely to give their money if he lets you skip out."

"He's not letting me; I'm going on my own. And I'm going now. So I suggest you get on with your duties."

"A pleasure!" Nigel yelled, jumping at Earl and toppling him backwards onto the stone steps. In a second he was sitting on Earl's chest, pinning him with his muscular weight. "And one of my duties is keeping upstarts like you in their place."

Earl flailed helplessly. A foot knocked the lantern into the snow, where it hissed and guttered out. Jumping from above, Welly and Heather set on Nigel, beating with their fists. To shake them off he partway stood. In a flash Earl brought up his arms. He grabbed the front of Nigel's coat, catapulting him over his head, through the doorway and onto the flagstones of the hall.

Quickly Welly spun around and shoved the door closed. No sooner had it thudded shut then they heard Nigel's furious yells for help.

"So much for escape by stealth," Earl said, starting at a run for the orchard. "You two had better stay behind now."

"Not us!" Welly said for the two of them, as he and Heather raced to keep up. "We're in this together!"

six

CLASH AT SUNSET

THE THREE FLEEING FIGURES HAD NEARLY REACHED THE outer wall, when the door behind them burst open. Lights and angry voices spilled out.

Seeing the high wall ahead, Welly squeaked, "What do we do now? This is a trap."

"No, there's a way over," Earl yelled. "I've used it before."

A dead tree, pale as a ghost, splayed against the foot of the wall. Earl leaped onto its gnarled trunk and reached a hand down for Heather. "There're footholds, chinks between the stones."

He boosted Welly up after her, then scrambled up himself. Crouching on the top of the wall, he looked back. Several lantern-swinging figures were coming their way, though clearly they had not seen exactly where their quarry had gone.

Agile as a cat, Earl leaped into the snow beside his companions. "Let's move!" he whispered, then pushed off through the drifts with the others slogging in his wake.

When out of earshot of the wall, Heather said, "In the

morning even a blind beggar will be able to follow the trail we're leaving."

"That's why I'm heading for the road. The snow there will be too packed for us to leave tracks."

Welly, both shorter and fatter, was having trouble keeping up. "Good idea," he said, panting. "But where to then?"

"Thinking of the old mines. Lots of ruins; good places to hide."

"What about the bloodhounds?" Heather asked. "They can follow people anywhere."

"Those are creatures from old books," Welly said confidently. "They don't exist anymore. Besides," he added for effect, not having the slightest idea if it was true, "dogs can't smell in the cold."

They slowed up for Welly. There was still no sign of pursuit. Soon they struck the north-south road and made better time. In the silence of the night, their boots crunched noisily over the hard packed surface. Perpetual overcast gave a gray tint to the sky. Against it, they saw the dark ruins of an ancient building. Jagged walls jutted like an upward-thrusting hand.

"There's the mine building," Earl said. "There are house ruins east and south of it."

"Think there'll be any muties or fell-dogs?" Welly asked anxiously

"Doubt it," Earl replied. "It's too close to town."

"Well, let's pick a house we can find again easily," Heather said practically, "up at the top of the hill."

They trudged up the road until it crested and dropped into a darkened valley beyond. There they left it, striking off to the east along a ridge. To Heather, the mine building seemed an ominously brooding tower. Not that she needed the fantasy, she realized. This adventure was proving exciting enough.

They approached the base of the building. "Careful of the shaft," Earl warned. "The other ruins are this way."

Soon they'd crawled into a refuge. Crouching behind one wind-breaking wall, they discussed plans. Originally they'd thought that once Earl was settled, the other two would sneak back and be innocently in bed by morning. Nobody would connect them with Earl's disappearance. Then the next night they could spirit some supplies out to him.

But now, when they went back, they'd probably be confined to their rooms with extra attention from the monitors and no chance to get out for days. The only alternative seemed to be staying with Earl the following day. Then they could sneak back, raid the kitchen for supplies, and deliver them the same night. After that, they'd have to return and face the consequences; but at least Earl would be provisioned until things blew over.

The night was well on now. The excitement of their flight drained away, and exhaustion took its place. Moving into the back of the ruined house, they found a corner relatively dry and shielded from the wind. There they curled up against a wall, pulling heavy coats close around them.

Sleepily, Heather recalled that in most adventure stories, fleeing heroes usually set someone to watch for enemies. But it really did seem a lot of trouble. Adventurers should be flexible, she decided, as she drifted to sleep.

When they awoke, it was mid-morning. Gray-white daylight seeped through the broken walls. Welly sat up, brushing his coat free of snow. The first thing he realized was that he was hungry. The second was that there was depressingly little he could do about it.

But Earl was already up, rummaging through his pack. "I brought along most of the dinner Heather got me last night. We'll have some sort of breakfast anyway."

Sitting in the feeble sunlight in front of their refuge, they shared bread and cold chunks of turnip. When they finished, Earl started repacking, but realized he was only putting off what he had to say. He turned to the other two.

"I don't know how to apologize for dragging you both into this. I should never have let myself impose on you."

"Nonsense," Heather began. "You couldn't know we'd get caught or that . . ."

"No. The risk was too great. I had no business involving other people in my problems—particularly friends."

Heather shook her head. "That's the sort of people you're supposed to involve in your problems."

"But now you're both in real trouble."

"That's the chance we took," Welly said. "The times you helped us, you took risks. You could've been chewed up by those dogs, or beaten up by Nigel."

"Besides," Heather added, "nothing terribly bad can happen when we finally go back. Not as bad, anyway, as you think going off with that Aunt Maureen would be."

Earl shivered at what the name invoked. "I wish I knew who she really is and what she wants with me. But I don't dare find out!"

He began pacing nervously. "It's as though the answers I want are the bait to a trap. She could tell me, but if I get close enough to ask, she'll catch me."

"Are you sure she's *not* your aunt?" Heather asked after a minute. "I mean, there is a resemblance, same pale skin and dark hair."

"Oh, we're tied up somehow, I'm sure of that. But she's not my Aunt Maureen. That's all wrong. And so is that Garth fellow. Very, very wrong." Sighing, he sat down on a section of the wall, his thin shoulders slumping forward.

Heather stood up and said briskly, "Well, anyway, you're free of them both now. They probably showed up at the school bright and early, put eveyone in a dither, withdrew their offer to old Greenhow, and left in a huff. As far as they know, you could be anywhere."

"Tomorrow after we're back," Welly said, "I'll get pen and paper and write a letter you can take to my family in Aberdare. They always need someone to help around the place, and it'll be a good spot to lie low until something better comes along."

Heather nodded. "Good idea, Welly. Your people seem decent enough to take him in. At least they want you back, soldier or not, after your schooling. Mine don't want me, or any friend of mine. They wouldn't care if they never saw me again."

She kicked angrily at a lump of snow. "You know, Earl, you might be lucky not knowing your family. Then you can fantasize anything you want—a home where you're needed, loving people who'd miss you."

"Maybe," Earl said. "But if I'm going to imagine relatives, I'll start with something a lot better than Aunt Maureen and Uncle Garth."

The rest of the day passed in talking, thinking, or dozing in patches of hazy sunshine. Gradually the bright smear of light that masked the sun moved toward the western horizon. Except for themselves, the silence on the hilltop was complete. Once they saw some sinuous animal dart into another of the ruins. But otherwise they might have been the only living beings in the world.

They'd been sitting in silence for some time when Heather suddenly jumped up. "I forgotten about Yule. It's tomorrow. Oh, and I bought you both little bags of candied chestnuts. I wish I'd brought them along!"

"So do I," Welly agreed wistfully.

"Ah, but that reminds me," Earl said. "I did bring your gifts. I never took them out of my coat pocket." He stood up, and after fishing around, carefully pulled out two small parcels.

"I hope you don't mind having them a day early. I probably won't see you tomorrow." He handed Welly his gift. "It's nothing to eat, I'm afraid."

Slowly Welly unwrapped the scrap of cloth and rolled the smooth white chess piece onto his palm. It was beautiful, a figure in rare ancient plastic, its shape delicate yet strong.

And it was a knight—as he was in fancy and had hoped to be in fact. Welly was surprised to find his eyes misting. He blinked and looked up smiling.

"I thought it was right for you," Earl said. "But I've never given a gift to a friend before."

Heather leaned forward to look at and touch the figure, white and cool on Welly's dark palm. Then Earl handed her the other gift. With a delighted squeak, she quickly unwrapped it, then paused as she held up the ring with its faceted gem. Even in the dull light it sparkled.

"It's beautiful, Earl," she said at last. "I've never had anything like it."

Earl smiled with the succes of his gifts. "You deserve beautiful things, Heather. Happy Yule."

"Oh, look. There's some writing inside."

"It says 'Cracker Jack,'" Earl said. "Though I'm not sure what that means."

"Hmm, Cracker Jack." Heather mused a moment. "That's right! I once read an old book where all the kids were always saying it. 'This was Cracker Jack,' or 'Gosh, that's really Cracker Jack.' I think it means all right."

"Good," Earl said. "Then it is a good luck charm. Thought it might be. So now maybe all you need do to make things all right is chant 'Cracker Jack.'"

Heather laughed. "Even in books, magic is seldom that simple. I think the real charm is that you gave it to me. Thank you, Earl." She blushed a little as she slipped the ring onto a dusty finger.

It was nearly sunset when Welly stood up, tucked the chess figure deep into a pants pocket, and said. "All right, let's launch this campaign! Now I suggest, Heather, that you and I leave here as soon as it's dark. We go right past the mine building to the road and along it until we come to the town wall. Then we can just work our way along that until we—Earl, how do you know the place to get over?"

"That old tree has roots right under the wall. You'll see

one sticking out of a bank. And there're footholds on that side, too."

Earl walked to the house's eastern wall and stepped around the corner. "This house is the closest to the mine building and right in line with the tower, so you shouldn't—"

He froze. Turning to them, his face was drained of color. "She's coming."

The two scrambled to join him. "No, stay back!" he hissed. "They've seen me, but they needn't know you're here."

Heather slipped inside the house and peeped cautiously over the sill of an eastern window. It was the same woman, all right. She recognized the black cape and hood. At first she thought the figure beside her was a dog, and she wondered if she hadn't been right about bloodhounds. But when she looked again, she saw it was a man.

"How did they follow you?" Welly whispered. "They're cutting across country, not even using the road."

"One more thing I don't know," Earl answered tautly. Then he stepped away from the wall. "Seems I can't run any more. I'll have to face her. But you two stay out of sight, no matter what."

Deliberately he walked away from the house and uphill toward the shattered mine building. Moving quickly to another wall, Heather and Welly peered out a shadowed north-facing window.

Earl stood waiting. At last two other figures moved into the framed scene. The sunset-tinged sky and blackened ruins hung as a backdrop.

"Well, young man," the woman said as they approached. "You certainly led us a merry chase. Why did you run away?"

"I decided not to go with you."

"That was a foolish decision. Your Uncle Garth and I run a very profitable business. Since it's our duty as kin to take care of you, we've decided to bring you into it. Right now, we're setting up a new operation in Wessex." She gave him a sidelong glance. "You'll like Wessex; it's run by a real king. And you do like kings."

"It depends on the king. Just as liking relatives depends on the relative. And anyway, I don't believe that you are my aunt, for all that you're as washed-out as I am."

"A perceptive boy, isn't he, Garth?" She frowned at her companion, then looked back at Earl. "All right, you deserve the truth. I am not your aunt. But we have known each other a long time. And you're a very important person, Earl. Or at least you can be, with our help. Think of it, Earl, I can help you learn all the things you've forgotten, all the things you've been trying to learn. I can help you find them, and much more. You'll have power, and I can show you how to wield it!"

"No! I don't want power—not through you. If I've got things to learn, I'll learn then on my own, or I'll be content to be a shepherd."

"You, a shepherd?" The woman threw back her head and laughed, a melodious, chilling sound. Her hood fell away, tumbling black hair about her shoulders. "Foolish boy, I know you too well. You could never be content with that. You need power, and you need us!"

Earl stepped back, his voice rising in intensity, "No, I don't need you. Get out of my life!"

"But I need you!" Striking like a snake, the woman jumped forward. She clamped his wrists in strong white hands.

Alarmed, the children watched the silent struggle. In the deepening dusk, it seemed that sparks actually burst between them, as though steel were striking steel. Garth watched from a distance, crouching, almost growling with excitement.

The two twisted backwards and forwards as Earl fought to break free. Suddenly he lunged backwards, pulling himself away. He staggered, swayed for a second, then fell from sight over the edge of the mine shaft. A terrible, long scream dropped away. Abruptly it ended.

Garth ran up the hill, and the two looked down the dark opening.

"Well," the woman said finally, "that's one solution. And perhaps it's the best, considering everything." She straightened up and turned away from the shaft. "Still, I could have used him."

"If you could have controlled him," Garth added.

She flashed him an angry look, shaking the tousled black hair from her face. "I could have controlled him—as long as his memory was gone. But still, if he ever got that back . . . Oh well, none of it matters now. It's over. Finally over."

"What about the body?"

"It's safe enough down there. But, with him, I should perform some laying rites."

"Now?"

"No. In this case, the dark of the moon would be best."

"That's night after tomorrow."

"Good. We can wait in town until then."

The two began walking along the ridge toward the road when the woman stopped and turned. Throwing back her head she thrust her arms into the sky and laughed. "All this time! All this time, and, at long last, I'm finally rid of him!"

Inside the ruined house, the two children sat frozen for long minutes after the others disappeared. Then, shaking, they stepped out of the house and walked slowly up the slope. At the top, they knelt in the churned-up snow and peered into the gapping shaft. "Oh, gods," Heather whispered. "I can't believe it."

After a moment, Welly said dully, "We ought to bury him, you know."

"Yes, I don't know what awful things that woman was

planning, but we can't let her have him. Let's go down there now.''

"There's some candles in . . . in his pack." Welly couldn't bring himself to say the name. How was it possible his friend was dead?

In the deepening twilight, Welly walked down the slope to the house, returning minutes later with two candles. Lighting them with flint and steel, he gave one to Heather. Together they explored the top of the shaft.

"I think there's a way down here," Heather said after a minute. "It's sort of slumped, and there're old timbers and machinery. We should be able to scramble down."

"It sounded like he fell a long way," Welly commented. "But let's go."

With much sliding and scraping, the two worked their way down, clinging to cold lengths of rusty cables that coiled down the wall of the ancient shaft. The feeble glow of their candles did little to light the monstrous shapes and cavernous holes looming everywhere around them. Dully, Heather wondered about goblins and trolls, but kept climbing down and down.

Finally, below them, they saw the body. It lay sprawled on a mound of snow and dirt, its dead eyes staring at the patch of sky far above.

Heather's sob echoed through the shaft.

❖ seven ❖

AWAKENING

HEATHER AND WELLY DROPPED THE LAST FEW FEET TO THE floor of the shaft, walked toward the body, then froze. The head turned toward them. Slowly Earl sat up, a calm smile spreading over his face. "Children!" he said.

"Children, indeed!" Heather snapped after a dumbfounded pause. "As if it weren't childish to scare us like that?"

They ran to him. "Why aren't you dead?" she asked.

"Sorry to disappoint you."

"No, I mean . . . You know what I mean!" She couldn't decide whether to hit him or hug him.

"I fell partway and got caught in those rotten ropes and things." He pointed up to where the faint candlelight suggested a tangle of shapes. "Knocked my breath out, but it broke the fall. Then something gave way, and I dropped down here. I hit my head and blacked out." An already purpling bruise on his right temple proved the last point.

"Oh," she said, sorry again, "does it hurt?"

"No. I mean yes, it hurts, but that's not important. What *is* important is that when I woke up, I remembered!"

"Remembered what?"

"Everything!"

"You mean, like who you are!" Welly asked excitedly.

"Yes, everything!" He threw back his head and laughed, a great upwelling of joy and relief. The peals echoed and reechoed through underground passages.

He stopped and groaned, pressing a hand to his head. "You really shouldn't laugh after cracking your head."

"So," Heather said, sympathy vying with impatience, "you know why that Maureen woman was after you."

Earl's smile faded. "Yes, all too well. And I also know how lucky we've been to escape her. Afterwards, did she say anything about her plans?"

"Yes, she did," Welly said. "They're going to come back and perform some rites over you."

Earl laughed flatly. "She would. Very thorough. But when, when are they coming?"

"It was night after tomorrow night, wasn't it?" Welly said.

Heather nodded. "That's right. She wanted to do whatever it was at the dark of the moon, and that creepy Garth fellow said it was in two nights."

"Good. Then we've a little time. She won't be happy when she finds I'm not here. So by then I'd better be as far away as possible."

He stood up, suddenly swaying. Welly caught at him. "Steady now. You think you can climb out of here?"

Earl stared up the dark shaft. "Probably. But we don't have to. There's an easier way."

"How do you know?"

"I know a lot of things now."

"So are you going to tell us about them?" Heather asked, exasperated.

"When we're out of here. It'll take a lot of telling." He stood a moment, as though listening to the darkness. Then he turned to his left. "This way."

He strode off into the gloom, and with candles flickering, the two hurried after him.

Earl led them into a low passageway. In places the earth was still held by ancient timbers, but in others, soil and rockfall nearly filled the passage. Several times Heather was on the verge of protesting, but whenever their way seemed blocked, Earl considered a moment, then found some gap that just let them through. At one point the passage divided into two. One way sloped down to the right, the other climbed steeply to the left. Earl stood, eyes closed, then chose the less promising right-hand route. Heather bit her tongue and wondered if they could find their way back again. She thought about the Minotaur and wished she had a ball of yarn.

After fifty feet, the down-sloping passage leveled then slanted up steeply. The candlelight glinted off curtains of ice clinging to the walls. Underfoot, the ground had the hard crunch of frozen mud. The air was heavy and deathly cold, but it moved faintly, flickering their candles as they continued to climb.

Earl had been walking ahead of them, almost beyond the circle of light. But now they came up to him, at what appeared to be a total blockage of the tunnel.

"Now what?" Welly asked. "Turn back?"

"No, there's space up there," Earl said, pointing upwards. He began hauling himself up the pile of timber and rock. The two younger children looked at each other. Heather shrugged and followed Earl.

Welly felt queasy and whimpery. He hated tight, closed-in places. But as Heather's legs disappeared into a dark opening, he knew he hated being left alone more. In panic, he scrambled up to where the passage shrank to scarely a foot high. Flat on his belly, he pulled himself along with hands and knees.

His candle brushed against a mud wall and snuffed out. Heather's body ahead of him blocked most of her light. He could feel the tons of earth above, waiting to shift and crush the life out of him. He wanted to scream! But the noise might loosen the dirt. When he stopped moving, the sense of weight was unbearable. Clammy with sweat, he kept crawling, following Heather's ever-receding feet.

Suddenly the feet were gone. Cautiously he stuck out a hand. Nothing but air, fresh cold air. Ahead, the tunnel widened and rimmed a patch of lesser darkness. They had come to another entrance.

Hands reached up and helped him down over a tumble of rock. Heather relit Welly's candle from hers and turned to Earl. "I hate to nag, but while you're explaining everything, you will tell us how you happened to know that simple little route?"

"I'll try," he said. "First let's find someplace to rest. Then you do deserve some explanations."

Not far from this entrance, they found a crude stone shed. Seeing nothing better, they checked the dark recesses for lurking animals and crawled inside. Blowing out the candles, they sat huddled together in the darkness, the doorway a gray patch in front of them.

"Well?" Heather said after a minute.

"I'm not stalling," Earl said. "I'm just not sure how to begin. You may find this little hard to take in."

"Earl Bedwas, Master of Suspense," she said sarcastically. "For goodness sakes, will you tell us?"

"All right, let's start this way. Do either of you know anything about Arthur Pendragon?"

"Arthur Pendragon?" She paused a moment. "You mean King Arthur? What can that—?"

"Just tell me, either of you, what you know about him."

They were silent. Then Welly said, "Well, he was a king in Britain who ruled after the Romans left. I think he's supposed to have united a bunch of little kingdoms and fought against whoever was invading at the time. The Saxons, maybe?"

"Good. Anything else?"

Heather spoke up. "I read a book full of tales of King Arthur a few years ago. It was pretty good, but I didn't like it as well as Robin Hood. The writing was too hard."

"What was it about?" Earl prompted. "Who were the main characters?"

"Well, there was Arthur, of course, very noble and all. And there was his queen, Guenevere. She had an affair with one of the knights and caused a lot of trouble. Lancelot, I think it was. And there were a bunch of other knights too, having adventures and going on quests. I forget all their names."

"Anyone else?"

"Well, there was some witch, who kept messing things up. She had a funny name."

"Morgan."

"Yeah, that's right, Morgan."

"Any other main characters?"

"Hmm. Oh yes, there was an old wizard named Merlin."

"And what became of him, in the end?"

"I don't remember really. Oh yes. Didn't he get bewitched by some other lady and shut up in a cave or something?"

"Yes, that's about it."

After a long pause, Heather asked, "So why the folklore lesson?"

"The thing is," Earl said slowly, "I've only been Earl Bedwas for seven years. For a long time before that, I was Merlin."

The two sputtered wordlessly.

"Don't ask any questions. Let me try to get this out first."

They fell into silence, and he began. "I was born about two thousand years ago. I won't go into the details of my life. Let's just say that it was recognized I had a good deal of power. I spent years studying magic and gradually gained some skill in it. Eventually I became advisor to King Uther."

Earl stopped and looked at Heather. "It's funny. I read those same stories, maybe five years ago, and they were just stories to me. Now it's as though there are two people inside me, seeing things from two different places. One of me sees those stories as interesting folktales, and the other sees them as garbled accounts of events I lived through.

"But still, the core of the stories is fairly accurate, though a lot of garbage has been added. King Uther did have a son, Arthur. For political and magical reasons, he was very important and in great danger. I took him away and saw to his upbringing in secret. When he was old enough, he was revealed as heir and king.

"But there were those opposed to what Arthur and I were working for. Some of the British kings were jealous; and of course, the Saxons didn't want Britain united. And then there was Morgan."

"The witch," Heather blurted out.

"Heather," he said severely, "witch is not the right word. Magic was more present in the world then. It comes in waves, I believe, throughout human history. Then we were at the end of a strong phase. Even common people had a little magic—skills and sensitivities that tapped into magical forces. Some of these might be called witches. But the term is not right for Morgan. She was a magician, a sorceress of great power. Such power often runs in families, and we were distantly related. Though," he added with vehemence, "she is not my aunt!"

"Maureen! You mean she—?"

"Let me finish, or you'll never make any sense of this. Morgan had her own plans, and they involved gaining control of events by playing sides off against each other and keeping Britain disunited. Every step of the way, she tried to thwart Arthur and me. And eventually she won, at least partially.

"For years, Morgan had been preparing an attack on me. Nimue." He paused for a minute. "Even after two thousand years, it still hurts." Sighing, he continued. "It was subtly done. Morgan knew my weaknesses. I didn't realize that Nimue was one of Morgan's creatures. Eventually I shared with her enough of my secrets that they turned my power against me. She and Morgan trapped me in a mountain and bound it about with enough spells to last as long as the mountain did. Which, of course, was the flaw. They didn't expect the mountain to be half blown away a mere two thousand years in the future."

"But, Earl," Welly interrupted, "Merlin was an old man, and you're fourteen!"

"You've noticed!" Earl laughed. "But think about it. Magicians are mortal human beings, powerful yes, but not gods. Even with all my powers—and I still had command of most, except those to break Morgan's spells—even with all that, I still aged. Eventually I would die. The path of magic I'd chosen gave me no command over death. That's where evil magic gets most of its strength: it has dealings with death. I imagine that's how Morgan has weathered these years; she's somehow suspended death.

"But, in any case, I didn't have that recourse. I did, however, have some power over time. And locked away all those years, I learned to slow it down, or at least slow its effects on life. And then I discovered how to reverse it. When I grew so old that death must be near, I reversed the flow and gradually grew younger. I grew younger until I reached the age when, if I went much further, I wouldn't have the skill to stop. Then I reversed it again and gradually aged.

"By the time the mountain was blown open, I had worked through several cycles. I'd gone through a turning not long before and was on my way up again. The explosion tore open the mountain and shattered Morgan's spells. But it also dealt me enough of a blow to completely bury my memory. It left me a helpless seven-year-old, with no idea of who I was."

"And the language?" Welly asked.

"That was just normal fifth-century British. I was always good at languages, so I learned modern English quickly. And since the older language had no memories to stick to, it just slipped away. I remember it now."

"Oh, and your name!" Heather exclaimed. "I bet you tried to say Merlin, and all the masters caught was the 'erl' sound."

"Probably. I'm pretty hazy about those early days."

"Earl . . . Merlin . . ." Welly began.

"Earl Bedwas has been a good name these seven years. Let's stick to that for a while. But before you ask me any questions, let me ask you one. Do you believe me?"

They were silent a moment. Then Heather ventured, "Well, believing things is never a problem for me. But really accepting them is something a little different."

Earl chuckled. "If someone had told me this story a few days ago, I'd have had trouble deciding if this latest fall had jogged his memory or addled his wits. But there were clues, I realize now.

"When I lost my memory, I lost all of it, including how to control magic. The power was still there, but untapped— except in stress or danger. Then it came out instinctively. And that scared me. I knew some things happened differently with me than with other kids, but I tried denying it to myself. That time in the snow, though, was the worst. I used the magic instinctively to escape, and almost died not knowing how to reverse it. Afterwards, I didn't understand what had happened, and it frightened me—a lot."

Welly frowned in thought. "You mean like when you hid behind the door from the monitor?"

"Yes. I tried to tell myself, and you, that he just didn't look carefully. But, in fact, I'd wished myself invisible so intensely that I'd become so. It's all a matter of manipulat-

ing the forces around you and the other person's mind. And
I did it automatically."

"And the fell-dogs and fighting with Nigel?" Heather
said excitedly.

"The fell-dogs, yes. There was more in my howling than
just noise, though I didn't know it. There was command.
But I don't think much magic slipped into my fighting. We
were taught to fight well when I was a kid—the first time."

"So what are you going to do now?" Welly asked.

"I don't know. This has all come back so suddenly, I need
to do some thinking. But in any case, I have to get away
from here, and soon, before Morgan returns. Do you two
think you can still slip back to the school and get some
provisions for me?"

"You can't just make food, now that you've got your
magic back?" Welly asked.

"Nothing nutritious. I sustained myself in that mountain
only through a web of spells and almost complete inactivity.
But magicians are just people; normally we've got to eat
just like anyone else."

"Pity," Welly said. "I was sort of hoping you could
spread out a banquet here. Sure, of course we'll go back. I
think there's still enough night left."

Heather agreed, and soon the two were climbing the hill,
past the ominous mine shaft and on to the road. For a while
they walked in silence, then Welly asked, "Do you believe
him?"

"Yes, even if it makes me sound as crazy as he does.
Remember how that Maureen or Morgan or whoever was
talking tonight? All about power and how important he was
and how she needed to use him? I thought maybe he was
some sort of lost heir and she wanted to be the power behind
the throne or something. But, really, this makes much more
sense—more if you remember all the strange things he's
done; the ones he's mentioned, and the way he got us out of
that awful mine."

"Yes," Welly agreed. "And remember the sparks. When he and that woman fought, it was like two swords clashing."

"So, you believe him, too?"

"Heather, I don't have the imagination you do. I don't take in weird things easily. But this is too real to be weird. I guess that means I believe."

The night was well advanced when they reached the school wall and the old gnarled roots marking the way over. But there were still several hours before the late winter dawn.

Already aching from their climb down the shaft, every muscle protested as they scaled the wall. On the other side, the two slipped quickly through the orchard toward the darkened bulk of the school. They were almost to the back door when a shadow peeled away from other shadows and leaped at them, gripping their arms.

"I thought you two might come skulking back tonight." Nigel's voice hissed. "I'm not on duty, but I couldn't pass up a little healthy revenge."

"Let us alone, Nigel!" Welly demanded, surprised at his own vehemence. "We didn't do anything to you."

"Certainly, I'll let you alone, as soon as I get you to Master Greenhow's room."

"Well, go ahead then," Heather said. "You've caught us, and we can't help where you take us. So it'll be *you* Greenhow yells at for waking him to report fugitives that'll still be here in the morning."

Nigel was silent for a moment. "You really aren't important enough to wake anyone for. And you're already in for a delicious punishment. He's furious at that ungrateful friend of yours for escaping. His aunt was beastly mad, scared the daylights out of old Greenhow and didn't leave him a penny."

He jerked the two children toward the back door and into the darkened hall. Immediately Welly's glasses fogged up, and he stumbled blindly as they turned into the girls' wing of the dormitory. "Let's stable you first, Horseface." Nigel laughed. "I brought along the extra keys."

They were hauled up a flight of stone stairs and along dim, silent corridors. As they neared Heather's room, Welly, who'd been mentally discarding one plan after another, whispered loudly. "This is sure a fix we're in. I'd sure like to see our friends Marian and Robin about now."

Nigel stopped at a door, thrust it open and pushed Heather inside. As he unhooked a ring of keys from his belt, Welly coughed and said emphatically, "I'd sure like to see good old Tuck right now."

Comprehension dawned on Heather's face, "Oh, look out!" she exclaimed. "My giant roach has escaped! Grab him!" She threw herself on her hands and knees just in front of Nigel. Welly smashed against him from behind, sending Nigel toppling over Heather onto the floor. Leaping onto Nigel's back, Welly pinned him down, while Heather whisked a blanket off the bed and wrapped it around his head. Then, snatching a belt and scarf off the back of a chair, Welly tied his prisoners wrists and ankles.

Nigel's yells were only mumbles through the blanket, but as Heather shut the door she whispered, "We don't want to smother him. Try a gag." She threw Welly an old undershirt for the purpose. Then, lighting a candle, she hastily stuffed things into a backpack, all the blankets, warm clothing and candles that would fit.

"Don't forget the candied chestnuts," Welly reminded her.

They dared say little in Nigel's hearing, but as soon as they slipped out the door and locked it behind them, Welly whispered, "I assume you're thinking what I'm thinking?"

The started down the corridor as she replied. "About burning our bridges behind us?"

"Right. Having Master Greenhow mad at us is one thing. But bashing and humiliating the nasty-tempered heir to

Glamorganshire—well, this isn't going to be a healthy place for us."

"I was sort of thinking we should go with Earl anyway," Heather said.

"Me, too. But this clinches it."

They hurried to Welly's room, where he quickly packed his rucksack. Then they slipped down to the kitchen. "We'll have to hurry," Heather whispered. "The kitchen help will be starting the fires for breakfast soon."

She led them to the pantry, and they began stuffing their packs with bread, turnips and even several sausages and lumps of cheese. "We'll eat like kings," Welly said.

"If we ever get out of here. That's enough now, hurry."

Welly crammed a heel of bread into his mouth as they slipped to the pantry door and cracked it open. Outside there was a shuffling. Lids clanked, and someone yawned by their door.

Welly's heart sank. He wondered if they'd be trapped in there all day. No. Someone would come into the pantry after something, and they'd be caught. He desperately wished he could do Earl's disappearing trick.

Then they heard a door open and close, and there was silence. "She's gone out to get more water," Heather whispered. "Hurry!"

They shoved open the door and glided like ghosts through the kitchen and down dark, twisting corridors. Once they hid behind a corner while someone sleepily stumbled by. Finally they made it to the back door and slipped into the pre-dawn gray.

Dawn itself was silhouetting the broken mine tower as they finally crested the hill. Briefly, they stopped at the ruined house, where they'd first hidden, to pick up Earl's pack. Then they worked their way downhill to the small shed.

They found Earl sitting in front, leaning back against the old stone wall. He was staring into the light along the eastern horizon. As they approached, he turned, giving them a blank look, which slowly changed into a smile. "You were a long time. Did you have any trouble?"

"Trouble personified," Welly said. "Our good friend, Nigel. But we put him in his place."

"Doubtful. There's not a place in Llandoylan bad enough for him." He eyed their two packs. "Looks like you've brought enough for an army. I don't know if I can carry all that."

"You needn't," Welly said crisply. "We're coming too."

Earl sighed. "I was afraid you'd say that." When they started to protest, he continued. "I'll admit, before you left, I almost wished you'd offer to come along. But now . . . now I just don't think I can let you."

"Why?" Heather asked. "What's changed? We're sworn to you and mean to follow through."

"I'll tell you what's changed. The world's changed! While you were away, I experimented with some magic, simple stuff. I hadn't really done much since I was sealed away. But things went all wrong, horrendously wrong. And I think I know why."

They looked at him, expectancy tinged, he thought, with skepticism. He sighed.

"Magic is a natural force, with its own laws, like gravity or magnetism. The force lines of what we call magic are part of all things in the universe. People with the power and training can learn to tap that force and use it. But like magnetic fields, it seems, magic changes over time. The lines and patterns of force shift."

Heather and Welly both wore slightly confused frowns. Earl continued. "That's the problem, you see. The force lines changed over time; but caught as I was in that web of spells, I didn't change with them. I'm no longer in tune with the patterns. I still have the power, but outside of close personal magic, like protection or finding the way out of that mine, everything I do is off somehow, out of kilter."

"Is that a big problem?" Welly asked.

"Yes, it is!" Earl said, his voice high with frustration. He jumped to his feet. "All right, I'll show you. I can still do personal magic, like changing my appearance, say."

He stood before them, and as they watched with growing amazement, his chin began to darken and he started growing a beard, a long, wavy beard. It looked a bit odd on a fourteen-year-old face, but it and the mustache were very impressive. Except for the color.

Earl looked down. "Purple! I can see I need to brush up on details. Well, no matter."

The beard shriveled and faded away as he turned and pointed at a good-sized rock some six feet in front of them. "But now, let's try this. Ordinary telekinesis is pretty basic stuff. I should be able to look at that rock and manipulate its forces and those around it until it lifts into the air. But watch!"

With his arms crossed, he stared at the rock, head tilted slight, face taut with concentration. Expectantly, Heather and Welly watched, but nothing happened. Then, gradually, they became aware of a faint buzzing noise. They turned to see a huge hornet's nest floating through the air toward them. It was aimed directly at Earl's head.

"Duck!" Welly cried. Grabbing Earl's arm, he yanked him to the ground.

The hive sailed over their heads and smashed on the rock he'd tried to lift. From the shattered pulpy sides rose a cloud of angry hornets. They swirled about undecidedly for a moment, then descended on the three watchers. In seconds, they were swatting, ducking and waving their arms frantically.

Earl spat out a singsong phrase. The hornets and broken nest turned purple.

"Damn!" he exclaimed. "Purple again!"

"Never mind the color!" Welly wailed. "Just stop them!"

Earl muttered something else, and the smashed hive burst into flames, consuming a number of hornets that hovered about it.

"Ah, that's better," he said and then groaned as the flames slowly melted down and coalesced into a large cream pie—distinctly purple.

This new arrival, however, interested the hornets. Soon, those insects not destroyed by the fire were swarming over the pie and sinking into its sticky surface.

"Well," Heather commented as the last hornet buried itself in the purple froth, "at least it got the job done."

"I can see," Welly said, "that this is going to be an interesting trip."

⊞ eight ⊞

QUEST'S BEGINNING

EARL SHOOK HIS HEAD. HE LOOKED AT HEATHER AND WELLY sitting against the stone wall, stubborn looks on their faces and full packs at their sides. "It would be all right," he said, "if it were only a matter of being interesting. But this trip will be dangerous as well. If I had my powers intact, we needn't fear the dangers of the road. Wizards travel in great security."

"But it's no different than if we were traveling with just plain Earl Bedwas," Welly pointed out. "We just have to deal with danger as best we can."

"True," Earl admitted. "And if we only had regular dangers to worry about—animals, brigands and weather—maybe we could chance it. But suppose, when Morgan finds out I'm not lying dead in that mine, she sets out looking for me. Suppose she unleashes a man-eating griffin, and I fight back with a cloud of butterflies—purple ones?"

"Maybe griffins are allergic to purple butterflies," Heather offered.

"What Heather is saying," Welly said before Earl could

sputter a reply, "and I am too, is that we're coming. So you might as well stop arguing."

Heather smiled impishly. "And if you try to stop us by turning us into rocks, you'll probably get a pair of panda bears as companions, or fleas maybe."

Earl laughed. "And they'd be purple no doubt." Running a hand through his hair, he paced in front of the little hut. Then he stopped and looked at them. "All right. Come along. You might be in as much danger if you went back to the school. Morgan knows you left with me, and if she learns you've returned, she might pay you a visit." The thought made the two of them squirm. "But remember," Earl continued, "you can drop out of this venture any time. Things may well get over our heads."

The two jumped to their feet. Earl grabbed up his pack and said, "Let's redistribute our gear. But not here, the smell of that cream pie is turning my stomach."

They repacked on a cluster of rocks upwind from the faintly buzzing pie. "Just one question," Welly asked as they shared a wedge of bread. "Where are we going?"

"I was thinking about that while you were gone. And the answer's inescapable. I've got to go find Arthur."

"King Arthur?" Welly said incredulously.

"But he's been dead for two thousand years!" Heather protested.

"Perhaps," Earl admitted. "I don't know. I was entrapped before that last battle so I wasn't with him. But, if you notice, the legends don't say that he died. They say he was gravely wounded and carried off to Avalon."

"Ah, that's just a fancy way of saying he died," Welly stated.

"No, it's not. Avalon is real. It's part of Faerie, a world parallel with ours and touching it at points. The folk of Avalon, the Eldritch, are interested in our world and occasionally mix in its affairs. And they always had a particular interest in Arthur. They prophesied his birth and kingship and gave him his sword. It seems likely that when all his work was collapsing and he dying, they spirited him away to heal and wait."

"Wait for what?" Heather asked.

"Wait until he was needed again. Until our world needed someone with Arthur's dream and his skill to bring it about."

Earl finished his packing and sat on a rock. "Maybe that's why I was released when I was. If ever there was a time when Britain needed a man like Arthur, it's now. A world blasted by human stupidity, with petty kings fighting each other and mutants invading its shores. And to add to that, evil magic seems to be loose. So, I'm afraid the answer's obvious: I helped bring Arthur into his kingdom before; that must be what I'm to do again."

A moment's silence. "All right," Heather said, standing up, "where is this Avalon?"

Earl gestured helplessly. "I don't know. The entrances, the places where the two worlds cross, change constantly. Who knows where they are after two thousand years, if there are any left at all? This world may be too dreadful now for Avalon to want any contact with it."

"So where do we go?" Welly asked.

"South, south and west. I feel that's the way. Maybe once I'm closer, I'll sense something. But, you see, this is a rather slender set of threads to hang on, so if . . ."

Heather stood up. "We're going, Earl, no more arguing." She shouldered her pack. "And we're going south."

They trekked off across country, sometimes talking, sometimes in companionable silence. Heather, tired as she was, glorified in every moment of it. This was adventure. This was a real quest. And it was something of her own. She wasn't needed at home; she wasn't needed at school. But maybe, just maybe, she was needed here. The hope thrilled her so, it frightened her.

Tossing her head, she let her hood fall back. Thin brown hair fluttered in the breeze. The sky was unusually clear, the sun almost a disk. In its diffuse light, the snow sparkled and glittered like crushed diamond. The white was blindingly lovely and the shadows a deep cool blue. How she'd love to have a gown like that, glittering as she walked, swirling into folds of mysterious blue. Her hair tumbling about it, pale and gold as the sun. How beautiful she'd be. All the world would see how beautiful. She sighed blissfully.

By midmorning they were tired, and hungry. Under a shelf of slatey blue rocks, they sat down and shared a hunk of bread and tangy sticks of sausage. Ceremoniously, Heather brought out the candied chestnuts. "Happy Yule," she said, doling them out. She'd only been able to afford a few, but they savored every crumb.

As they finished the meal, Earl cleared his throat uncomfortably. "I'm not a maker of sentimental speeches. But I want you to know I appreciate your sticking with me."

"But we're friends," Welly said simply.

"That's what I mean—you're friends. I've had very few in either life. I never admitted to myself that I needed them. That was my real weakness, and Morgan knew it and used it. That's what she's best at, playing on people's weaknesses until she breaks them and turns them to her will.

"She knew I needed someone like Nimue, and so she trained her and insinuated her into my life until I was trapped by my own need. But for all that, I don't blame her; Nimue, I mean. She herself was trapped by Morgan. And despite everything, I loved her."

Earl was looking off into the distance, as though seeing over time as well as miles. "During those long years, I often wondered what became of her, once she had served Morgan's purpose. I hope she broke away and found peace somewhere."

He sighed and stood up. The three shouldered their bags

and set off over the silent landscape, their breath rising in plumes against the cold air. After a while, Welly asked about Garth.

"That creature?" Earl replied. "He's not from the old times. You can tell by his darker skin for one thing. His ancestors mutated for survival."

"Oh!" Heather exclaimed. "So that's why you and Morgan . . ."

"Are so washed out?" Earl laughed. "Our ancestors lived well before the Devastation. Then most Britons were pale as we are, though people near the equator had lovely dark skin like yours, or darker, to filter out the sun.

"But Garth," he said, returning to the subject, "is of your world, though his mutations may have taken some nasty turns as well. Morgan usually picks deeply flawed creatures for her lackies. Her evil can get a firmer hold on them."

Welly was frowning in concentration. "Earl, something just occurred to me. Remember the night someone broke into Greenhow's office? Do you suppose it was one of those two—looking for your records?"

"Hmm. From what you saw, I think it could have been. They must have found the mountain destroyed and rumors led them to the school. And . . . and that time in the snow. I'm not sure if it was a deliberate trap. I don't think so." He shivered. "If they'd known about my memory then, they could have caught me easily."

In midafternoon, they joined the south-running road and luxuriated in its packed surface. On either side stone walls snaked over the hillsides in shadow-rimmed ridges. Ancient in origin, they now marked fields where hardy mutated crops grew in the brief summers. Some fenced livestock, whose ancestors had been among those few farm animals which, sheltered during the Devastation, had not died of cold or radiation.

Sunset was still an hour off when Earl gestured toward a

cluster of trees and ruins on a ridge to their west. "Let's stop and set up camp. None of us got any sleep last night; and I, for one, am exhausted."

Welly and Heather, who had been walking the last several miles in a mechanical stupor, mumbled agreement.

They struck off along the ridge, on what had once been a road. It led to a grove of dark pines, in the midst of which nestled a ruined chapel. In one far wall the delicate stone traceries of an arched window were still etched against the shrouded sky.

"We're going to spend the night here?" Heather asked dubiously, eyeing the tilted gravestones in the low-walled churchyard.

"It's shelter," Earl said, then noticing the focus of Heather's attention, he added, "I wouldn't worry about ghosts. I doubt that spirits who knew the old world would bother drifting into this one."

They stepped through the broken archway. The roof over the back was still intact. Under it, they swept pine needles into a nest beside the stone altar and spread their blankets over them. Then, leaving Welly to select provisions, Heather and Earl gathered fallen branches and built a fire in the roofless space where pews once stood.

As the sun set, the fire blazed up, postponing the dark, which Heather still did not quite trust here. Three split potatoes were stuck into the fire's edge. While these cooked, they nibbled on bread and turnips.

"We're certainly eating a lot better than at school," Earl observed, "thanks to our resourceful, light-fingered provisioners."

"We did our best," Heather said. "I just hope Cook doesn't get into trouble."

"She won't," Welly assured her. "It wasn't her fault the kitchen was hit by thieves. No, I imagine once the scandal dies down, the whole place will get along quite well without us."

"Scandal!" Heather breathed excitedly. "Well, at least I'll have made some impact on those beauty queens. Just think, someday we may be school legends!"

Welly snorted. "Yeah, the three misfits who forsook their inheritances and took to the wilds."

"Some inheritances," Heather and Earl said together and laughed.

The fire was dying down, and they were thinking comfortably of sleep when a noise outside jerked them alert. A sound of shuffling. Two ragged figures stood in the doorway.

"Well, well, look what holed up here," drawled one. "It beats knocking people off on the highway, when they just sit and wait for you."

The other laughed. "Now, didn't I tell you, Tom, we should bed down here? There ain't no ghosts or Druids, just plump pickings."

They pushed their way into the firelit chapel, followed by three others as ragged and surly looking. Heather and Welly shrank back, eyes wide with fear.

"That one's nice and plump anyway," one of the newcomers observed.

"Save that sort of thing for your mutie friends," Tom spat. "We'll go for the clothes and provisions."

"We can take the girl for the slavers," one suggested.

Tom grinned. "Or maybe for us."

Earl stood up, breaking the stunned silence of the intended victims. Something in his bearing halted the bandits' advance. "We have no money and few provisions," he said calmly. "And we are not for sale. So I advise you to leave and find pickings elsewhere."

"Oh, indeed?" Tom said. "Well, I'll tell you something else about yourselves. You're three children, and you're unarmed. Come on, boys!"

The five bounded forward. Earl thrust one hand down toward the fire. It leaped from smoldering embers into tall

flames. The sudden new light lit the bandits' startled faces:
With another gesture, Earl sent the fire hurtling off from the
ground.

It shot up like a meteor, but in the wrong direction. The
three children threw themselves to the flagstones. The fire
hurtled over their heads in a shower of sparks, hit the back
wall and ricocheted off. The brigands yelped as the fire-
ball swooped toward them. Suddenly, it jerked upward,
slammed into a tall pine and extinguished itself. The con-
cussion snapped off a branch. This crashed down into the
chapel, pinning one of the attackers beneath it.

Amid shrieks and yells, the others ran off, pausing briefly
to drag their companion free. For several minutes they
heard the highwaymen's cries fading into the distance.

Earl sat down, feeding another branch into the remaining
embers. "I'll have to work on that fire trick a bit. But at
least it wasn't purple."

That night they set watches. One sat wrapped in a blanket
by the fire while the other two slept. The wind wailed
forlornly through the darkened trees, and the two younger
children kept a particularly attentive watch in the direction
of the graveyard. Snow began falling during the second
watch, but nothing more disturbed the night except the
distant cry of a rare and lonely owl.

✖ n i n e ✖

DRY SEA'S CROSSING

AFTER BREAKFASTING IN THE CHAPEL ON BREAD AND DRIED radishes, they repacked their bags and set off. Heather hardly gave the graveyard a parting glance. In the light of morning, the gray markers behind the wall were just stones without the slightest mist of menace about them.

Wind had whipped the night's snow into frothy drifts, which, they noted, would cover their tracks from the mine. As they stepped free of the grove, Earl stopped for a moment, looking south to where the land dropped away below them. "We're almost to the shore," he said dreamily.

"Shore?" Welly questioned.

"There used to be a great arm of the sea down there, the Bristol Channel. Now you can't even see it from here.

"It's odd," he continued after a pause. "To Earl Bedwas, that was just another geography lesson. But now I remember the Channel. I sailed across it between Cornwall and Wales. I can close my eyes and see the sparkling water, the white caps and blue sky."

"Well, if we're heading that way," Welly said, "I'd

rather walk than sail. I've only seen enough open water to wash my face in, and I haven't any idea about swimming."

Heather objected. "Oh, Welly, I can't believe you don't yearn to see the ocean. Why half the ancient books talk about it! There's always so much adventure there: pirates, and smugglers and romantic ladies walking the shore."

Welly grunted. "Well, our romantic lady will just have to be happy with a dry road, because that's all there is."

They walked on through the morning. Unlike the day before, Earl said very little, answering the occasional question in short, distracted replies. At last Heather asked, "Is there something wrong, Earl? If you're worried about last night, don't. Your fire business was a little indirect, but it got rid of them."

"No, that's not it. I'm sorry I'm not better company. But seeing that seascape, where there wasn't any, set me to remembering. This used to be such a beautiful world. So different from now. I can't even describe it to you."

Head lowered, he continued walking. "If our world had been destroyed by a great flood or by a piece falling from the sun, that would be fate. But to find that we destroyed it ourselves, that hurts."

He strode along in silence for a moment, then suddenly turned to Welly. "Remember our talk in the library? Something about it kept bothering me, but I couldn't catch it. Now I know. You said you loved strategy for its own sake. But remember, it's only a tool! I think that's one thing that went wrong. People got so involved with their clever tools and strategic thinking, they were blind to everything else."

The route they were taking was an old one, which once ended in the east-west coast road. That thoroughfare could still be seen, but modern tracks ran alongside to avoid its broken pavement. From the intersection, a new road continued south, built over the years more by human feet and carts than by engineers. It stretched before them across the former channel, a gray strip on a white landscape.

Around noon, they passed six merchants on their way north to Wales. They were armed and traveled with two laden pack ponies. Ignoring the stares of surprise at their own vulnerability, the children warned them of at least one band of brigands ahead. Otherwise, the day was uneventful, and the night was passed among a cluster of large rocks not far off the road.

Earl took the first watch, wrapped in a blanket and leaning back against a boulder. Welly cocooned himself in blankets on the opposite side of the fire, but sleep did not come easily. He lay with his eyes open, watching the thin banner of smoke curl up into the night. Finally he propped himself up on an elbow.

"Earl, I've been trying, but it's hard to imagine what this must be like for you. I mean, it's like every kid's fantasy. I used to think how great it would be, to know what I do now and be, say, a toddler again. And now you sort of have that."

Earl grunted. "Well, yes, I know the fantasy. And sure, I remember my life before; but after two thousand years, memories lose something of their immediacy. Besides, what I remember applies to people and situations in the fifth century. It doesn't help much here."

A coal popped and leaped from the fire. Earl kicked it back with the edge of a worn boot. "And something else, age affects more than how your body looks; it changes your thoughts and feelings. In most ways, I really am a fourteen-year-old." He paused, then laughed wryly. "I've been remembering how trying it was being a teenager before. And now I have to go through it all again!"

"Oh, come on," Heather said from the fire-reddened darkness. "Everyone's always moaning about the dreadful teens. Surely it's not as bad as all that."

"No, maybe not." He grinned at them. "At least I now know that 'this too shall pass.'"

In the morning a brisk wind had risen in the west, but there was no new snow. Patches of ice were dotted about, rimmed with dry reeds, which clattered like bones in the wind. Here and there the ground was blown clear of snow, revealing the coarse curly grass and a new plant, thick, blood-red succulents that grew close to the ground and made wet popping sounds when stepped upon.

Late in the afternoon, a long glimmering line that they'd seen in the distance resolved itself into a river. "The River Severn," Earl announced. "It just followed the retreating sea, cutting itself a new bed in the silt."

As they approached it, they saw that only the river's edges were gripped in ice. The central channel still flowed freely. A bridge had been built a century or so earlier by rolling large stones into the water and spanning these with timbers and building scraps. The whole structure looked rickety and in need of repair. Earl stopped short of crossing it.

"Do you think it's safe?" Heather asked.

"I'm sure it'll hold us. That's not what worries me."

"What then?"

"Trolls. Wherever there's a bridge, one has to consider trolls."

"Oh, come on!" Heather complained. "That's only in stories. It's just a bridge."

"The stories of one time are based on the truths of another. And quite a few things seem to be cycling back. Still, we have to cross."

He led the way onto the bridge, but when he reached the first splinter plank, he tromped heavily upon it and chanted. "Troll, troll, under timber and stone, we cross this bridge although it's your own. We cross with your leave and our blessings you'll take, we cross without it and a cursing we'll make."

The two younger children could barely keep from laughing as they followed Earl onto the creaking, sagging span. But they were only halfway across when a horrible little mannekin swung up from under the railing and landed squarely in their path.

The creature was small and hunched, with long arms and bowlegs, his body covered with splotchy yellow fur. His head was bald and wrinkled, with a thin yellow beard that began at the huge splayed ears and ran under a receding chin. He glared at them out of small, close-set eyes.

"You take my cursing instead," he lisped wetly. "And me grind your bones to make my bread!"

Earl laughed. "You're new at this, aren't you? Now stand aside, we're going over."

"It's my bridge!"

"Agreed, and we're crossing it."

The troll gurgled hatred and leaped at Earl, filthy claws outspread. Earl ducked and grabbed the creature around the waist. The troll wiggled like an insect as Earl lifted it over his head and tossed it into the roiling river.

He turned to the other two, wiping his hands on his coat. "Didn't have to use magic on that one. Good thing too, or I'd probably have burned the bridge under us or turned it to pudding."

As they continued across, Heather looked back over the rail to see a bald head bobbing downstream. Finally a bedraggled yellow creature pulled itself onto the bank they had left. It shook both fists at them, but its words were lost in the water's rushing. Heather was glad that at least it hadn't drowned.

The cloud-smeared sun was already low above the western horizon. As they stepped off the end of the bridge, Earl stopped and surveyed the barren land ahead. "Let's camp here for the night. It's near water, and this road would be too easy to lose in the dark."

"But what about the troll?" Heather asked.

"I doubt that he'll bother us again."

They built a fire of grass and bits of driftwood as twilight fell about them. The blaze filled the air with a pungent tang and flushed their faces with heat, forcing them to occasionally turn about, like spitted meat, warming one side and cooling the other.

As they ate supper of bread and hard cheese, Heather asked, "Was that really a troll, Earl, like in stories, or just a mutie?"

Earl though a moment, feeding knots of grass into the fire. "That's not an easy question. Old-time trolls mutated from something, too. They were creatures of Faerie. And I guess that since the Devastation, some doors between this world and the other have opened wider. That young fellow back there may be part of both. He knew some of the traditional forms anyway."

Heather frowned. "Why didn't those merchants warn us there was a troll at the bridge?"

Earl laughed. "He probably didn't show himself to them. They were six grown men and armed."

They stacked their fuel near the fire. Then Earl and Heather curled up in two hollows, but Welly, a blanket draped over his shoulders, sat by the fire keeping the first watch. All had passed uneventfully when he wakened Earl for the second watch, and after several hours Earl woke Heather for the last.

With one blanket about her shoulders and the torn half of another wrapping her cold feet, she huddled close to the low fire. To her left, she could hear the steady gurgle of the river. Occasionally, over it there were other sounds, ice cracking along the edge or the distant cry of some wild animal.

Whenever she heard the latter, she was tempted to drop

more fuel into the smoldering fire. But she'd found that a bright fire nearby turned the grayness around her to black. With the glow reduced to a few red coals, she could see farther into the night. She hoped fervently there was nothing out there to see. But in case there was, she wanted to see it at a distance.

Slowly she fed twigs into the embers. The glow spread a soft circle of light just beyond the sleepers.

She looked at them fondly. They were so different. One round and soft-looking, the other all edges and angles. Yet her heart warmed to them both. They were her friends. What did they see, she wondered, looking at her when she slept. Angrily she twisted her braid, dismissing the thought. She knew the answer all too well. But she wished that, lying there alseep in the firelight, she could be beautiful for them.

A rustling noise snapped her back to attention. She stared into the darkness and saw a darker shape, which had not been there before. With flapping and creaking, it moved closer. She was reaching out to wake Earl, when the creature spoke.

"It's Troll. Me hungry. You have food?"

"Yes, and it's ours," she replied, with more bravery than she felt.

"It was my bridge, and you crossed it."

"You didn't build the bridge."

"You didn't bake the bread."

She paused a moment. "How do you know?"

"Me clever troll. Also hungry troll. You give bread and me no eat your bones."

"No. I might give you bread because you have no bones to eat. But you won't have our bones in any case."

They watched each other for a minute. The troll's beady eyes stared from a face both sad and grotesque. Keeping her eyes on him, Heather leaned forward and fumbled through a sack for a piece of bread.

The other's thin, spindly body hunched forward hopefully

in the cold. Slowly she unwound the old blanket from her feet. Wrapping the bread in its folds, she threw the bundle out to him. A squeak and shuffle and he was gone.

She saw and heard no more of the creature. Soon the sky began graying in the east. When it was light enough to see the bridge, she woke the other two, but said nothing about the night's visitor.

The three washed themselves in the river, or washed as much of themselves as they could stand exposing to the cold. Then they ate a light breakfast by the ashes of the fire.

As they were packing up, Earl heard a reedy whistle behind him. He turned to see the troll squatting on a rock twenty feet away. He was wearing an old torn blanket as a shawl. Earl glanced at Heather but said nothing.

Addressing the troll, Earl said conversationally, "Going to be stopping any more travelers today, do you think?"

"Depends."

"On how few and weak they are?"

"Well, me a bridge troll! How else do me make a living?"

"Oh, guarding bridges is fine, if it's your line of work. But there are ways to do these things."

"Such as?" the troll replied sulkily.

"Well, great big horrendous trolls can threaten to grind people's bones. But little ones have to be cleverer."

"How?"

"The usual thing is to ask riddles. That way, if they guess the answer, travelers know they've earned a crossing. But if they don't, they feel you've earned a toll. You'll get more food and things that way, even if you don't grind many bones."

"Hmm. Me like riddles. But don't know many."

"That will give you something to pass the time between travelers, making up riddles."

The troll mumbled and hissed in a thoughtful sort of way, then slid off the rock and disappeared.

Earl stood up, shouldered his pack and said loudly, "If everyone's ready, let's go."

Welly was down by the river, stuffing his pack with bits of driftwood for future fires. He hurried back to join them, and the three walked off toward the road, followed from behind by a pair of beady eyes. At Heather's sleeping place by the dead fire lay a carrot and the end of a sausage.

The day was like the one before, except that as the morning passed, Earl began feeling more and more uneasy. He kept glancing to either side and behind them, but saw nothing. Heather felt it too, though nothing seemed to be following or watching them. But the feeling grew.

Once Earl noticed a pair of birds circling high in the cloud-layered sky. At one time he would have thought nothing of it, but in this world birds were not common. He kept a wary eye on the winged shapes floating silently overhead.

The ground began sloping up as the channel road rose slowly toward the former shore of Devon. In midafternoon, they stopped to rest, sharing a handful of roasted barley. Heather leaned wearily against a rock. She'd been walking so long that her legs felt as if they were still swinging and pumping ahead. She wondered dully if they'd ever finish walking.

As she mechanically chewed her barley, her interest was caught by a thin gray line at the edge of the west-sweeping plain.

"What's that?" she asked Earl. "Clouds?"

He squinted into the west. "No, it's the ocean. The Atlantic Ocean."

"Oh, I do hope we get a chance to see it closer sometime."

Just then, Welly called from where he'd been exploring ice-clogged pools on the other side of the road. "Hey, come look what I've found!"

The two pushed themselves off from the rocks and,

crossing the road, scrambled down the far bank. There, half encased in mud and ice, were the rusted remains of an ancient device.

Welly kicked at one pitted silvery strip. "I think it's an automobile, or one of those mechanical carts."

Earl poked around, studying the parts. "You may be right. But how did it get out here?"

"Yeah, I was wondering that," Welly replied. "Maybe it fell off a ferry boat."

"Or maybe," Heather suggested, "after the Devastation, when all the fuel was gone, people hitched horses to it and used it as a cart, until it got stuck out here."

"Yes," Earl said, straightening up. "Maybe. But we'll never know. Let's be on our way."

They turned back to the road, but stopped short. Leaning calmly against the rocks where they'd just rested were Morgan and Garth.

"Earl, dear," the woman said, "I'm so glad you weren't hurt by that nasty fall at the mines."

"Cut the charm, Morgan," Earl said flatly as he climbed back to the road. "We both know who we are, so you needn't waste your sympathy."

"Ah," she said, smiling slyly at her companion. "We thought you might be remembering when we heard about highwaymen running into a skinny kid who threw fire."

Heather gasped. She hadn't thought of that giving them away. The sound shifted Morgan's attention to her, and for a moment the woman stared at her with thoughtful green eyes.

"Well, Morgan," Earl said, drawing back her gaze. "If all you wanted was to renew old acquaintances, you've done that. I can't say that even after two thousand years it's been a pleasure. But with any luck, maybe we can avoid meeting again for another couple millennia."

"Dear Merlin, always your same charming self. I can't see how I've gotten along without you all this time."

"Try, because I'll give you another chance." He tried to move past her, but she stepped in his way.

"Blast it, Merlin, let's call a truce. Don't you see? The world's changed! All the causes and people you fought for are dead. Come with me now, and we can start afresh. We can remake this world the way we want it."

"Any world you made wouldn't be worth living in. No, Morgan, I'm through with that. You buried me away from my first life and destroyed everything I built. Now I don't want any more building. I just want someplace I can be left alone."

"Where are you going then?"

"I don't know. This world hasn't much left in it. But I'll find someplace." He motioned to Heather and Welly, and the three pushed past the woman and her silent companion.

"You'll regret not joining me, Merlin!" she called after him.

"I've regretted many things having to do with you, Morgan," he said without turning around, "but never that."

Heather felt eyes boring into her back as they walked up the road. But when, at the crest of the hill, she stole a backward glance, the two figures were gone.

"Do you think she believes you?" she whispered when they felt safe. "That you're looking for someplace to be a hermit, I mean."

"I doubt it. It buys us some time, maybe. But I expect we'll be hearing from her again."

Welly whistled. "I'd as soon not, thank you. I've never met a creepier lady."

"Not many people have," Earl said, "and lived."

They continued along the road. The west wind was stronger now, knifing into them with cold and damp. Stormlike, the gray line in the west was moving closer. The wind steadily picked up force, stinging their faces.

The three travelers pulled their hoods tight and staggered on against the gusts. Overhead, dark gray clouds streaked against the lighter sky. In the west, the gray band was much closer. Heather stared at it as they hurried along. From above came the thin cry of a sea gull.

Suddenly Heather stopped. Her voice quavered. "Earl, I don't think that's storm clouds. Look at it. That's water!"

The others stopped and stared. The gray line was no longer a distant smear. It was solid and drawing nearer: a great gray wall with flecks of white at its top.

"It's the ocean!" Welly yelled. "The whole ocean pouring back! Run!"

He and Heather bolted off the road, running east as fast as their legs would go. Earl stared at the approaching horror, then leaped after them. "Wait," he called. "Don't run!"

The wind ripped his words away. The two kept up their panicky flight. He increased his speed, pounding his long legs over the uneven ground. Finally, he was up with Welly. Lunging, he grabbed his arm. Dragging him along, he tackled Heather.

They all rolled together on the ground. Looking up they saw the towering wall of water sweeping down upon them, pouring over them. Water was all around, green and deep, pressing down on their lungs. Weird undersea shapes swept past.

I'm dying, Welly thought. I can't breathe! Beside him, Heather was flopping about, gasping helplessly like a landed fish.

Earl knelt between them, his dark hair streaming about him like seaweed. He grabbed them both roughly by the shoulders. "You can breathe!" he yelled. "It's just illusion. There's no water, just air. Breathe! Don't think you're dying, or you will."

Welly stared up at him, eyes wide with fear. Earl thumped his friend's chest. "Breathe! It's air! There's no water. Breathe air!"

Welly gave up and took a deep breath. He wanted Earl to be right. He wanted air in his lungs. And there was. He could breathe, although deep green water lay around and above him.

Earl was working on Heather now, hitting her on the back, urging her to breathe. Gradually, she stopped writhing and began to take quick, shallow breaths. Sitting up, she looked wonderingly about her.

"We can breathe under water?"

Earl replied firmly. "No, it's just illusion. There is no water."

"Are you sure?" Welly said, ducking as a twenty-foot-long, finned snake sailed serenely overhead. Smaller fish darted about in the glimmering water. Beside them, on the sandy ocean floor, feathery plants waved in the currents, and shelled creatures scrambled over slimy rocks.

"Look!" Heather said jumping up, her fear almost forgotten. "A ship!"

They looked up to the light-shimmering surface. A storm raged silently there, and a great ship tossed about on the waves. As they watched, the prow dipped under, and the whole ship upended and began a slow, deathly dive. The delicate shape was all grace and beauty as it spun downward. A few figures swirled from its decks and were carried off by the currents.

"That ship!" Earl yelled. "An Eldritch ship. Quick, run to it!"

He bounded off over the sea bottom, and the other two ran after him, dodging fish and clusters of barnacle-encrusted rocks. As Welly leaped over it, a many-armed sack recoiled and loosed an inky black cloud.

The beautiful ship hung nearly above them. Heather screamed to Earl to keep out from under it, as in eerie silence it settled to the ocean floor. Great clouds of green-gold silt welled up into the water, swirling around them, blinding them and dissolving at last into the wind and the weak afternoon sunlight.

Welly and Heather stumbled to their knees in what had been a cluster of sea anemones. The snow was cold and dry under their hands as they crouched, gasping and shaking their heads. They looked at each other. Their clothes weren't even wet. No seaweed dripped from their hair.

Welly began laughing, and Heather joined him, taking in great beautiful lungfuls of air. When the two finally quieted and dried their eyes, they looked up to see Earl standing above them, a relieved smile on his face.

"Quite an illusion, wasn't it?" he said.

Welly sat up. "I can hardly believe it wasn't real. I mean, it was all there. Did you see any of it?"

Earl sat down beside them. "Oh, yes, I saw it. But if you're trained, there are ways to tell illusion from reality. It was a beautiful job, though, technically superb. She must have been perfecting her talent all these years, because she never used to be as good as that."

"Could it really have killed us?" Welly asked. "Even if it was just an illusion?"

Earl nodded. "If a person's mind believes he's dying, then often he dies."

Heather frowned. "But if Morgan knew it wouldn't fool you, why did she try? Just to show off?"

"Well, there may have been some of that. But basically it wasn't aimed at me, I'm afraid. It was aimed at you."

The two looked startled. "But she doesn't even know us," Welly protested.

"No, but she's quite astute. She recognized that you two are important to me, so she tried to hurt me through you."

"Oh, that's fine," Heather said dryly. "Then we needn't take it personally that she tried to kill us." She stood up and was brushing snow off her knees when something occurred to her.

"Does she know about your . . . your little problem with magic?"

Earl shook his head. "I don't think so. If she did, she'd have gone at me directly by now." He scowled at his boots. "I suspect she's stayed in the world all these years and moved right along with its shifting magical forces. She may not even know that they have shifted. And, right now, her ignorance may be our best defense."

Welly stood up and readjusted his pack. "Well, I certainly hope she doesn't try another trick like that. It's incredible that it was all fake. The ship and everything."

"In a way," Earl said, "that part wasn't fake. That's where she went a little overboard, if you'll excuse the pun, in her obsession for accuracy."

"What do you mean?" Welly asked.

"Well, the first part, the returning sea, was all her creation. But the undersea part—I don't think she made that up. Such a complete illusion needs background detail, and Morgan probably hasn't spent enough time on ocean floors to store up all those images. What she did was call up images from the past. She clearly reached far, far back. You can tell by the sea serpent and the ship."

"Yes," Heather said, looking around them suddenly. "Why were you so anxious to reach that ship?"

"Because it was an Eldritch ship. And since those were real images, that ship once actually sank here."

"But so what?" Welly said. "I mean, who are these Eldritch?"

"You probably know the term Elf better—but they aren't pixies sitting in flowers! They're one of the races of Faerie. When our two worlds were closer, many Eldritch lived in this one. Even later, there was coming and going between them. My own family has Eldritch blood in it.

"I tried to see where the ship sank because I want to find the wreck. Come on. I threw my pack on the spot just before the illusion faded."

The two followed him to where the pack lay on a patch of snow-covered ground, indistinguishable from anything around it. Welly kicked at the snow. "Why exactly do we want to find this old wreck?"

Earl squatted down and spread his hands over the ground. "Because there are certain Eldritch things that would be useful to us now. Many of the materials they used are not affected by age."

He shifted his search to another spot. The others watched as their friend crawled over a large area of ground, face tense, the fingers of both hands spread like questing spiders.

Finally he grunted with satisfaction. "Here, this may be something." He stood up and kicked at the ground. "Wish I could use magic, but I'd probably melt everything. We'll have to dig."

He pried a rock from the ground and began gouging into the half-frozen earth. Heather and Welly did the same.

Welly was thinking they'd been digging forever when his rock struck something hard enough to send shocks up his arm. He poked and scraped at it until a metallic gleam showed through the dirt. The others joined him, and soon they'd unearthed the object he'd found and others stacked under it.

"Swords!" Welly breathed.

"That's what I hoped for. The Eldritch made wonderful swords with their own enchantments forged right into them."

"Magic swords?" Heather whispered.

Earl chuckled. "Not quite. At least they're not guaranteed to slay dragons. But even ordinary Eldritch swords have certain built-in protections and ease of use. And from our experiences so far, I'd say we can use some good weapons."

Reverently he pulled six red-gold blades from the ragged hole. Brushing away the clinging dirt, he spread them on the snow. "Choose whichever feels right in your hand. They serve masters best if the match is right."

Heather ran her fingers over the smooth, sunset-colored metal, and finally she pulled out a short, delicate blade with hilt carved like a flower-entwined branch.

Welly knew which he wanted immediately. He pulled out the sword with the pommel that ended in an arched horse's head, like the chess piece in his pocket. Earl's choice had a tapered crosspiece adorned with two hawk heads.

With the point of his blade, Earl poked around in the empty hole. "Ah, I thought there was something more."

Under the spot where the lowest sword had lain, he brushed away some of the loose crumbly earth. For an instant, Heather thought she glimpsed a small bag of wonderfully embroidered cloth. But at Earl's touch, it vanished with a puff of dust. Scattered through the dirt, though, was a sparkle of colors, a dozen faceted jewels of different hues and sizes. Scooping them up, Earl held them in the light, while the others gazed in wonder. They'd seldom seen real jewels, and these twinkled with a depth of color they'd scarcely imagined.

"These might be useful," Earl said as he fished his old coin bag out of his pocket. In a cascade of color, he poured the jewels into it, then returned the pouch to his coat. The three remaining swords he placed back in the hole and covered with dirt.

"We'll leave these for any who need them. Eldritch hoards don't respond well to greed."

Returning to the road, Earl and Heather gave Welly a wide berth as he swung his sword in great sweeping arches over his head. "Just let that Morgan try again!" he yelled.

"That sword won't be much use against her," Earl cautioned. "Though she may well try again. As soon as she decides what I'm really about, she's bound to."

"Doesn't she have any other hobbies besides harassing you?" Heather asked.

"Plenty, I imagine, and all unsavory. But as much as she hates me personally, I'm only secondary. If Arthur is brought back, it will definitely complicate her plans."

"Well, then," Welly said, brandishing his sword in the air, "let's go complicate them!"

ten

MIST ON THE MOORS

THE ROAD ROSE STEEPLY TO THE OLD DEVONSHIRE SHORE. IN the west, the sun slipped below the horizon. Above it hung the ghost of a new moon.

Ahead, on a prominence, lights shone out from a small settlement that had once been a prosperous fishing village. Tired and hungry, the three trudged up the road past the old stone quay that now jutted uselessly into the the dry night air.

With relief, they stepped onto the cobbled streets. Above the door of a large whitewashed building, a lantern-lit sigh swung in the evening breeze. "The Rose and Unicorn" was lettered neatly above a painting of the mythical beast entangled in a rosebush.

"Roses and unicorns." Earl sighed. "Both equally extinct."

He looked at his two companions a moment. "What do you say we spend tonight in an inn? One of the jewels should buy a warm meal and dry beds, which we deserve, I think, after our mental drenching.''

Heather looked excitedly at the glowing windows. She'd never stayed in an inn, but it was the sort of thing people always did in adventures.

The sign creaked merrily overhead as they stepped through the door. The customers sitting and talking at tables in the fire-lit common room automatically glanced their way, then continued staring. Even with their Eldritch blades concealed under their coats, they were an unusual sight. With brigands and slavers about, healthy, unmutated children did not travel the roads alone.

Ignoring the stares and sudden silence, Earl strode over to where a stout, aproned man was clearing trenchers from a table. The boy felt uncomfortably out of practice, but attempted an authoritative manner.

"My good man, we would like beds and a good meal for the night, and breakfast in the morning."

The landlord stopped his cleaning and looked Earl up and down. "Well, young master, you can have 'em, if you can pay for 'em."

Earl lowered his voice theatrically. "I have a jewel that is worth a good deal more than any room or board you could possibly provide. But as we can neither eat it nor sleep on it, we will give it in exchange for the very best you have."

The landlord's eyes were akindle, but he spoke skeptically. "Let's see this great treasure then."

Earl was prepared with a ruby already in his palm. He opened his hand and tipped the jewel onto the table. With a deft flick of a finger, he spun it like a top on the well-worn tabletop. The facets caught and spun off the firelight in kaleidoscopic flames.

Catching his breath, the innkeeper slammed a palm down on his prey. He held it up to his eye, examined it carefully and bit it. Then he bobbed his head at Earl and smiled ingratiatingly. "You shall have the best, young sirs and mistress. The very best." And he bustled off to the kitchen.

"That was fun," Earl said in a low voice as they took a table close to the fire. "I didn't have the gall to do that sort of thing the last time I was fourteen."

The meal lived up to the promise. They were served fresh milk and a large pie with both meat and mushrooms in it. At the school on a high day, they might have one or the other, but never both. There as a side dish of fried onions and the host even brought out a dessert—biscuits with a dollop of rare gooseberry preserves.

Welly and Heather agreed they'd never tasted anything so delicious as this last. Earl knew that he had, but since it was some two thousand years earlier, it hardly mattered.

After the meal, the landlord took them upstairs to their room. It was clean and cheery, warmed by the brick chimney from the common room below. At least half of the window panes overlooking the street were of real glass. A small rag rug lay on the plank floor, and the two beds were piled with reasonably fresh ticking and abundant blankets. It was clearly the best room in the house, reserved for travelers of consequence.

Earl dismissed the landlord, conveying that the room was acceptable but certainly no more than their due. Then, as soon as the man left the room, Earl set about defending it. It would clearly need defending. Here were three obviously wealthy children traveling unescorted and apparently unarmed.

Since the swordsmanship of two of the three was untried, Earl decided on a magic defense. If he could make it work, that would at least eliminate the need for setting watch.

A door guardian would be sufficient, he decided, since the windows were reasonably inaccessible. After opening the door and checking to make sure the hall was empty, he tried conjuring a guardian snake to coil about the door handle. What he produced, however, was a vase of daffodils. Heather exclaimed that these were really lovely, but Earl wasn't pleased. The next attempt converted the daffodils into an ostrich, which, though alarmingly large, was not suitably aggressive. Then in rapid succession they went through a tennis racket, a guinea pig, and a potato pancake. Earl was on the verge of hysteria when the next apparition proved to be a dozen large centipedes. He gratefully accepted these and set them about the doorknob and threshold with accompanying protective charms.

The effect, though not as impressive as the five-foot cobra he had aimed for, was none the less successful—judging by the yowls and retreating footsteps that disturbed them in the middle of the night.

In the morning Earl spoke the dismissing formula, and the three children watched their wriggling guardians puff into nothing.

Before heading down to breakfast, Welly said, "Earl, I think I should send some sort of message to my parents. They'll worry when they hear I've left Llandoylan. Even if I can't explain what I'm doing, I can let them know I'm all right."

Earl frowned. "Of course, you should, and I should have suggested it. I guess there's not much responsible adult left in me. We can get pen and paper from the landlord, and he can send the letter with the next traveler north. Heather, why don't you write your family, too?"

She snorted. "Those people don't need me. The one thing better than not having me home is not having me anywhere. But I'll write, even if only to make them feel guilty because they weren't worried."

After leaving the inn, they exchanged an emerald for food and a sack of coins. Earl considered using other gems to buy horses, but neither of the others had ever ridden a horse. And although the shaggy three-toed beasts were considerably lower to the ground than the ones Earl had known, they were also a great deal feistier. So rather than risk broken necks, they continued on foot.

At the edge of town, where an ancient stone pillar guarded the crossroads, they stopped to consider their route. So far, traveling by road hadn't seemed any freer from danger, either natural or supernatural, then traveling cross-country. So they decided to strike off straight southwest.

Not far from the crossroads, they knew they were being followed. Two men were strolling over the open country, parallel with them and keeping pace, although their longer legs could soon have put them well ahead.

Earl figured that one, at least, had visited them during the night; his hand was newly bandaged. Concluding that they might already be wavering in their intent, Earl turned and whipped out his sword. The two men consulted hastily. With casual menace, Earl moved toward them, his bearing suggesting he knew how to handle his sword far better than his age implied. The men turned, and a retreating walk soon broke into a run.

Smiling, Earl rejoined the others and stuck his sword back in his belt.

"Can you really use that thing?" Welly asked in awe.

"Riding with Kings Uther and Arthur, even a bookish wizard learned how to use a sword." He noticed Heather still looked doubtful. "Besides, I wasn't a dottering old man all the time, you know!"

The hillside soon led them onto the moor. With only a light snow cover and the ground frozen hard as stone, they made good cover. Their first two days proved uneventful except for occasional glimpses of wildlife: albino deer, birds and several feral cats.

On the third day, a stiff wind drove at them from the west. By afternoon it carried a fine dry snow, which sifted into their clothes and rustled over the ground like sand.

Toward evening they saw through the gusts of snow a cluster of tall stones off to their left. Welly suggested they shelter there, but Earl insisted such places were dangerous, though he didn't elaborate. So they passed the stones by, and looking back, Heather admitted that their stark shapes alone on the moor were vaguely unsettling.

They spent a cold, uncomfortable night huddled against a rocky bank. By morning, the snow had changed to large, wet flakes and was falling much faster. Eating a quick breakfast, they hurried on, hoping that movement would warm them. The wind blew with rising force. Snow swirled thickly in the air and piled the ground in deep foot-clogging drifts. Around noon, they stumbled upon a cluster of stone ruins, and Earl suggested they hole up there and wait out the storm.

The ruins were a group of circular stone huts set partway into the ground. Their domed roofs were largely gone, and in some the walls were broken away, leaving nothing but round, rubble-filled depressions. The whole site breathed an aura of great age.

When they had crawled into a hut more intact than most, Heather said to Earl, "I thought you warned us to stay away from ancient stone places."

"It was the circles and tombs I meant, the sacred sites. The ancients who built those dealt in powers we'd best avoid. But this was just a farm village."

Next day the storm was worse. It howled and shrieked outside their refuge, curtaining the air with white. Earl told stories of old kings and warriors and workers of magic. After a while he wondered if he told them to entertain the others or to comfort himself. Maybe Morgan was right. Maybe he was still tied to the old, dead world and had no place in this.

Angrily, he shoved the thought aside. Long storms always depressed him. He brought out his wooden flute and played lively warming tunes.

The next day the storm subsided around noon, but

temperatures dropped rapidly. Cold cut through their heavy clothes like keen-edged knives.

Earl had been struggling for several days to regain control over fire. He still wasn't able to start one from scratch. At times nothing happened, and at others he produced alternatives that were quite alarming. But once Welly had kindling started with flint and steel, Earl could now sustain it without further fuel. It was a small triumph, though, and a frustrating contrast to his former skills. Dejectedly he wondered if his power would ever be realigned with this world.

The following day proved even colder than the last. Every minute outside left skin tingling and painful for hours. Deep breaths drew needles of ice into their lungs.

The incredible cold, however, drove the almost perpetual murkiness from the atmosphere. Through the open roof, they saw above them a clear, icy blue. Heather kept leaning back against the stone wall and gazing up. A wonderful shade for eyes, she thought. Far better than the muddy shade of her own.

Much of that day Earl seemed lost in thought, apparently not cheerful thought. Heather took up the task of entertaining by telling stories she had absorbed in her constant reading.

One was an ancient tale of "How the Elephant Got His Trunk." None of the three had ever seen an elephant, and they weren't certain if it was mythical or merely extinct. Earl doubted the scientific validity of that method for altering a species' nose. But the story brought him out of his gloom.

Another story was "The Hound of the Baskervilles." Partway through, however, Heather realized that their setting gave this tale an uncomfortable reality, and she would have stopped if her listeners hadn't demanded to hear how it came out. They were particularly delighted when the great detective, Sherlock Holmes, hid in a neolithic stone hut on the windswept moors. But her vivid account of the chilling climax left them all listening for the sound of distant howling.

After several uncomfortable minutes, they submerged themselves in Heather's verbatim recitation of the tale in which "Pooh and Piglet Go Hunting and Almost Catch a Woozle." The resultant mood was more comfortable.

That night the sky remained clear. For the first time in their lives, Welly and Heather saw a whole sky filled with stars, unobscured by the lingering dust pall of the Devastation. There were more stars than they'd ever imagined. They glinted like chips of ice, crystalline and brittle, set in a bowl of deepest black. Heather thought that this one sight made up for all the hardships and dangers. She could hardly sleep for the beauty spangled overhead.

By morning, the high clouds had returned again, curtaining the sky. The air seemed less bitter. Eagerly the three shouldered their packs and emerged from the ruins, looking about them at the snow-covered world. It seemed criminal to plow into the sweeping drifts and mar the untouched whiteness that spread to every horizon. The fallen flakes, when they did step into them, were distant and feathery, and squeaked underfoot.

Going was slow, and not entirely because of the deep snow. Free from days of confinement, the three were bursting with exuberance. Heather and Earl took to diving into the deepest drifts and cavorting about like ancient sea animals. After carefully tucking his glasses away, Welly joined them. It felt very good.

They hadn't gone many miles from the huts when darkness confined them again, this time to an old stone sheep pen. Temperatures continued to rise through the night, and by morning they were in a midwinter thaw.

The snow became sloppy and less pleasant to walk

through. Its wetness soaked their boots and trousers. As the vast fields of snow began melting, mists rose across the moors. That night they were cold, wet and miserable, and by morning the mists had coalesced into a real fog.

Dank whiteness closed around them. Sky and ground became one. Only Earl's sense of their goal kept them moving in a straight line. At times the wind blew at the fog, tearing it aside for glimpses of bleak, silent landscape. Then formless vapors rolled around them again, deadening all sight and sound.

They trudged on, Earl in the lead, followed by Welly and then Heather. As she forced herself along, Heather tried to keep her mind as blank as the view around her. Otherwise she thought about being cold, wet and miserable. It was totally expected when a bank of slush sucked at a sodden boot and pulled it off. She groaned and sank into the snow the probe about with chilled fingers until she pulled her boot free. Tugging it back on, she dragged off her wet gloves and fumbled stupidly over the laces. At last she stood up and resumed her march.

But now she couldn't see the other two, not even a glimpse of a retreating back. She wasn't even sure in which direction she should look for them. Panic pricked her stupor, and she cursed herself for not having called out when she stopped.

She called now, but the sound seemed dull and muted, swallowed up in the fog. She tried again, louder, and thought she heard an answering call. Stumbling off in the direction it seemed to have come from, she called again. There might have been another answer, if it wasn't the wind, but it came more from the left. She shifted direction and labored on.

Her heart leaped. She must have been right. Through the shredding fog she caught sight of a shape, no, two shapes in the mists ahead. She hurried forward, sobbing in relief.

The fog closed, then swirled away again, and the shapes

were nearer. Only there were more than two. She slowed down and stopped. They were stones, tall standing stones, jutting from the ground like malformed teeth. Wisps of fog whipped around them, making them vanish and reappear as though part of a dance.

She wanted to turn and run in the other direction, but she didn't know which other direction was right. At least these stones were solid, and if she stayed here, she'd be at some fixed point. If she called, maybe the others could find her.

Hesitantly she passed between two of the looming gray shapes. She could see now that they were ranged roughly in a circle. Some were tall and erect, while a few tilted at crazy angles and others lay half-buried in the earth.

She stood waiting, calling from time to time. But the feeble sound didn't seem to reach beyond the stones. A numbing chill slowly spread up her spine. Something, she felt, was behind her. It was not her friends.

Clamminess, like a hand, clutched her shoulder. She tried to scream, but her throat was frozen. Her legs couldn't move. They were pillars of stone like those around her. Weakly she fought against heavy gray thoughts. The thoughts solidified around her, encasing her in their hardness. She would stand here in the cold forever. Millennia would come and go, stars would wheel overhead. She would be untouched, unchanging stone.

❈ e l e v e n ❈

REFUGE

HEATHER STOOD IMMOBILE, BLANK EYES STARING BLINDLY into time and space. At some meaningless point she saw a flicker of movement. It was passing, insignificant. There were sounds, too. Words perhaps. But what did they mean to her?

They came again, incessantly, beating on her. "Move," they said. "Move out of the circle."

Move? How could she move? Her legs were solid pillars of rock. The words were foolishness. But they came again, chipping at her solidity. And slowly her legs did move. They lifted and came ponderously down again. Closer to the edge of the circle. Yes, perhaps the voice was right. Perhaps she should move out of the circle.

The voice beat at her brain, thawing it. Warming blood pulsed through her body. The cold gripped tightly at her shoulder, tugging. But steadily she moved against it, cracking its hold. Another tottering step and another. She fell forward between stones, free of the circle.

Dazed, she rolled over in the snow. Earl and Welly stood over her just outside the stone ring, their swords drawn.

"Now!" Earl yelled, and both of them plunged their blades into a roiling column of smoke that hovered just beyond the gap she'd fallen through.

The blades met no resistance, but the shapeless form suddenly writhed and folded in on itself. A hollow, whispering sound, and the shape swirled away to the other side of the circle. It thinned and vanished on a gust of wind.

Returning swords to their belts, Earl and Welly helped Heather to her feet.

"Talk, sympathize, scold, whatever you want," she said weakly, "but let's do it away from here."

The fog was lifting now, all over the moor. With the two boys supporting Heather, they moved as fast as they could until the stone circle was hidded behind a ridge. Then gratefully they settled onto a rock, once Earl had satisfied himself that it was a perfectly natural and neutral rock.

After a long silence, Heather whispered, "That was the most evil thing I've ever imagined."

Earl squeezed her arm. "Foul maybe, but not really evil. Stone-wraiths aren't good or evil. They have their own rules. But they are very, very possessive."

Heather groaned.

For the rest of that day they were propelled by that horror behind. They caught sight of several other standing stones and a huge stone table, which Earl said had been a bronze-age tomb. These they earnestly avoided. The night was spent in the open, huddled around a magically sustained fire.

Just before morning it began raining. It rained on and off all day. Their clothes, though designed for cold and damp, were finally overtaxed. Now the children were constantly wet and chilled.

As the afternoon wore on, temperatures dropped slightly, turning the rain to sleet. Liquid ice poured out of the sky, solidifying as it hit. Soon the ground was covered with ice and treacherously slippery. Finally they took cover under a rocky outcrop where a skeletal bush gave the weak illusion of shelter. The icefall continued through the night, twice almost dowsing the fire. Toward dawn, it tapered off.

The sun rose on a new world. Everything was glazed with ice. As far as they could see, the moor glinted and reflected back the light of the sun like a rippled mirror. The bare branches overhead glistened like sun-touched jewels.

This beauty, however, was flawed. Walking was like stepping on wet glass. They could scarcely put one foot in front of the other without falling.

They hadn't gone far from the night's camp when Welly lost his footing at the top of a hill. He catapulted onto his back and, arms and legs flailing, shot down the slope. He reached the bottom and began yelling. Heather and Earl, fearing he was hurt, sat down and deliberately slid down the hill after him.

When they reached Welly, he was near hysterics. They gathered that in his wild slide, his glasses had flown off. Without his glasses, Welly was so helpless he could not even look for them. So he sat miserable and blind while Heather and Earl crawled up the glassy surface searching. At last, halfway up, Heather found them, a glint of metal and glass on a field of ice. They were unbroken.

The rest of the day was spent scrambling over the ice-slicked landscape. As the bruises and cold built up, tobogganing lost its appeal. When, in late afternoon, they made it to the top of another rise and saw an inhabited farmstead beyond, it was as though they had glimpsed paradise.

Heather stood for a moment gazing at the stone house, a gray column of smoke curling from its squat chimney. "I don't care if the place is peopled by a whole family of stone-wraiths. Let's visit."

"Wraiths don't need fires," Earl told her. "But at the moment, I'd hardly care if they did, so long as they shared."

In minutes, three bedraggled children stood knocking on the low wooden door. A shuffling inside, and the door cracked open. A man's bearded face, set in cautious curiosity, peered out at them.

After a second, he threw the door wide. "Martha, John Wesley! Come here; it's all right. It's rare we have visitors, but I can tell children needing a warm fire when I see them."

The three were hustled inside. Their sodden coats were removed, and they were plumped down on benches before the fire. They were just beginning to thaw when mugs of steaming hot soup were thrust into their hands. They drank eagerly while the farm family smiled and watched them.

Earl put down his mug. "Sir and Madam, I can't tell you how grateful we are to be taken in and fed like this."

"Well, it's only human charity," the man said. "And you looked like you could use it. But we're not 'sir and madam.' We're the Penroses. I'm Josiah, and this is my wife, Martha, and our son, John Wesley."

After their introductions, Welly's and Heather's eyes widened at Earl's account of how they'd gotten to the Penrose's door. "We all three were students at a school in Glamorganshire, but last month the school had a fire and had to close. Since Heather and Welly haven't any family, they're coming with me to my home in Cornwall. But we ill-advisedly took a shortcut over the moors and have had some rough days of it."

"I shouldn't doubt you have, poor lambs," the woman said. "But you'll stay the night with us now. We've extra bedding to spread by the fire. I don't imagine you've been sleeping too well out there, what with the cold and wet and the strange things on the moors."

"No, Madam . . . Mrs. Penrose, we haven't."

The motherly woman was soon bustling about, laying out extra ticking and blankets by the broad hearth. As she helped them out of their dank clothing, she commented,

"You may have to stay over with us an extra day just so I can wash your clothes. They're so stiff, they almost stand by themselves."

That night, sleeping dry by the fire, tucked into clean, warm blankets they seemed, indeed, very close to paradise.

In the morning, Welly woke up hot and shaky. Everything around him seemed oddly distant. Mrs. Penrose proclaimed that he was sick and shouldn't budge from his bed and that anyway it was a mercy they weren't all down with fever after what they'd been through.

Welly got steadily worse. For days his skin was hot and dry, and he developed a wracking cough. He swam in and out of consciousness, always followed by a swarm of images. There were smoky wraiths and trolls dancing on mountains of water, and a beautiful pale woman with black hair and green eyes who alternately offered him gooseberry preserves or ripped off his glasses and stamped on them.

Heather and Mrs. Penrose cared for him, keeping him covered as he thrashed about, bathing his forehead with damp cloths and making him swallow bitter medicinal concoctions.

Earl was worried for his friend, and he was toweringly frustrated. He had been a fair master of healing magic, but he was afraid to try it now for fear he'd kill rather than cure.

Heather noticed how glum Earl had become, and guessing the problem, she told him over and over again that he wasn't to blame. But he wouldn't be comforted. He was ashamed of his impotence, and for a time tried to avoid her, the one person who knew he should be able to help.

He threw himself instead into helping Josiah and little John Wesley around the farm. The Penrose lands were on the edge of the moor and, except for a considerable kitchen garden, were devoted to livestock. When the snow cover was light, the dark-wooled sheep, shaggy ponies and shaggier cattle were let out onto the moor. When it was heavy, or an ice fall sealed off the grass, the stock was kept in pens and barns and fed on the red succulents, or "blood-plants" the travelers had seen on their way.

"These are wonderful plants," Josiah told Earl one day as they shoveld the dried leathery pods into a bin. "The minister calls them 'God's Mercy on the Survivors.' They say that when everything else stopped growing after the Devastation, the blood-plants and moor grass just took over. The stock'll eat blood-plants dried or fresh, and they make fine fuel. When times are hard, people can eat 'em too, though if you ask me they taste like rancid pickles."

Working in the stock barn or on the moors, Earl often found seven-year-old John Wesley tagging along. The boy was small for his age. On one side, his arm was shriveled and his spindly leg was too short, giving him a rolling limp. Yet he seemed irrepressibly happy. He had no schooling and wasn't likely to get any. But he understood his world.

When the two were alone, Earl told the younger boy stories, some from reading at Llandoylan and others well-disguised adventures of his own. In return, John Wesley taught the things he knew, natural things that the wizard Merlin had known, but that in this world had changed almost beyond recognition. Earl learned the new weather signs, and the names and natures of those few new plants and creatures that had replaced the many old.

On his bed by the fireplace, Welly lay ill for a week. But at last the fever broke. He was tired and very weak, but the coughing was down to a rasp, and he could sleep without those fever-conjured companions.

His first real food was bread soaked in vegetable broth. Heather brought him a bowl and sat down by his bed to talk. She told him what she and Earl had been doing and about the little newborn lamb John Wesley had shown her.

Welly licked up the last drop in his bowl. "These folks sure've been good to us. Leave it to me to get sick and be a burden." He sighed. "I've held up Earl's plans, too. Is he mad?"

"No, not mad. Not at you anyway. But he's upset that he wasn't able to help you."

"Well, that's not his fault. He would've if he could. I'm not blaming him."

"I know. But convincing him not to blame himself is another matter."

Welly sighed again and looked down at his hands, plump and dark against the white sheet. "Well, something good ought to have come of this. But look, a week of not eating, and I'm as fat as ever. It's not fair!"

"Welly!" she admonished. "We're so happy you're better nobody cares what you're shaped like!"

Later that night as Welly was sleeping peacefully by the fire and Josiah and the two boys were out tending to the stock, Heather echoed what Welly had said and she had been thinking. "You know, Mrs. Penrose, you've all been very kind to us. There's no way we can ever repay you."

"Lord's mercy, child, you've been repaying us every moment you're here. If the Lord had allowed it, this house would be full of children. But that hasn't been His choice for us. We've only little John Wesley now."

The woman sighed. "I'm sorry you never met our older son, Charles. He was a good lad and strong. He was born healthy and stayed that way until he got the bone sick and right away died. Poor little John Wesley has had afflictions since he was born. So maybe that's enough, maybe he'll stay with us."

"I hope so, Mrs. Penrose. He certainly is a cheerful boy."

"He is, and he loves your Earl. Follows him around everywhere. Not surprising. That Earl is a fine lad and very bright. He's sure to make something of himself someday."

"He has . . . I mean, he has been told that."

"And he's been such a help around here. Since Charles died, it's been hard on Josiah, running this place. And you've been a help to me too, Heather, you know that."

The woman dried the last bowl and put it in the cupboard. "What I'm saying is that we've been very happy having you here. You can stay as long as you wish, and . . . and if any of you wanted to stay longer and kind of make this your home, well, that would be fine, too."

Heather felt her insides knot with yearning. This woman wanted her. She wanted her here to share this home.

Heather closed her eyes and swallowed a lump that had risen in her throat. "Mrs. Penrose, sometimes I think there is nothing I want more than to stay here. But we can't. Earl has things he must attend to, and Welly and I are bound to go with him."

"I know. You three are very close," the woman said with a sigh. "But think on it."

Welly's recovery was steady. After another few days, though still weak, he was walking about. Heather and John Wesley took him to the barn to meet the newborn lamb. Welly, seldom comfortable with animals, had to be coaxed to pat the wooly head. But once he had, the baby was soon licking mashed bloodplant from his hand. Its small pink tongue lapping his fingers was flannelly and warm.

At last Welly was well enough for the three to consider resuming their journey. But it was a decision that day after day they put off. There were things to do around the farm, and Josiah was showing them the basics of horseback riding. Conversation only skirted around their departure.

One afternoon, Welly was outside exercising his new vigor by shoveling manure into trays where it would be dried for fuel. The clouds were swollen yellow-brown with coming snow. John Wesley was in the barn trying to convince the lamb to wear and not eat the braided grass collar Heather had made for it.

Inside the farmhouse, Heather and Mrs. Penrose were rewinding tangled skeins of yarn. Seated on the floor in front of the fireplace, Earl and Mr. Penrose were repairing a broken yoke. As they worked, Josiah told Earl what he hoped to trade for this year when the roads to the market towns were passable.

Suddenly Welly burst through the door. Startled, they all looked up. "There's something awful out there!" he gasped. "It's got John Wesley cornered against the barn!"

Instantly Earl was out the door. He ran into the yard, but skidded to a halt when he saw what waited. The animal was the size of a deer, and slender. But its legs ended in wicked-looking talons, and its tail was long and whiplike. Short reddish fur on the body lengthened into a mane. Black eyes glinted from behind a cruel beak.

This was no natural mutation, Earl knew. There was something too bizarre, too intentionally evil about it.

The thing swiveled its head and gave Earl a cold, appraising stare. Then it turned back and continued its step-by-step advance toward John Wesley. The boy stood pinned with terror against the barn door.

Without pausing, Earl hurled a magic attack at the creature. The only effect was a strong odor of roses and a melted patch of snow. The beast kept stalking the boy. Earl tried again, this time producing only a sound—the jangled discord of a falling harp.

He screamed in frustration, and at least the creature stopped a moment and looked at him, beady eyes snapping in annoyance. Well, Earl decided, if all he had left were personal defenses, he'd use them as a shield!

Several bounding steps, and he stood between the creature and the boy. The animal crouched and opened its beak. Shrieking, it lunged at Earl. He threw up an arm, and the beast recoiled. Cautious now, it advanced more slowly, making little feints and jumps. Not turning around, Earl grabbed John Wesley's arm and moved backwards, always keeping the boy shielded. Hissing in its throat, the creature leaped again. The air cracked, and again it was rebuffed. Earl continued stepping back. The beast kept pace, lunging and snapping, but never closing.

The retreating dance went on and on until, behind him, Earl felt the barrier he sought. A waist-high stone wall ran across one corner of the yard, cutting it off from an old quarry hole.

Still clutching John Wesley behind him, Earl taunted the beast. He poked and kicked toward it. Reaching down, he grabbed a handful of pebbles and threw them at its face.

The eyes blazed. The creature hissed and rumbled ominously in its chest. Feigning indifference, Earl turned away and looked toward the farmhouse and the four people watching in frozen horror. Out of the corner of his eye, he saw the beast crouch. Muscles rippled under the smooth red fur. With a piercing shriek, it leaped at Earl's head. Instantly he threw himself and John Wesley to the ground.

The animal sailed over their sprawled bodies, its talons missing them by inches. The note in its cry rose sharply. It flailed the air, then tumbled into the rocky pit to lie twitching and broken at the bottom.

In seconds, the others were with the two boys, helping them up. Mrs. Penrose hugged her boy to her, muttering endearments. Josiah slapped Earl on the back. "I don't know how you did it, boy, but that was wonderful! You certainly had that creature fuddled."

Heather and Welly peered over the wall at the form splayed on the rocks below. Even dead, its strangeness made them shiver. They wondered what it had been or, more disturbing, where it had come from.

Mr. Penrose echoed their thoughts. "No question about it, that's the strangest creature I've ever seen, and we've known some odd things on these moors."

They took the boys into the house and fussed over them some more. John Wesley, rapidly rebounding, chattered about how wonderful Earl had been in fooling the "bird-cat." Earl said very little.

After supper, as Mrs. Penrose stood to remove the plates, Earl spoke up. "Mr. and Mrs. Penrose, I think the time's come for us to be on our way again, or at least for me to be on mine. We've been a burden to you long enough."

"Oh, lad, don't say that," Mrs. Penrose said, sitting down. "You've been anything but a burden. Why you just saved our boy's life!"

"But if I hadn't been here, his life would never have been endangered. You are good people, and this is a fine, peaceful home. But the longer I stay, the more of a threat you're all under."

Mr. Penrose cleared this throat. "Well now, I can't exactly see how that can be, lad. That mutie beast just chanced upon the place, drawn by the sheep, I should think, not by any of us."

"I can't expect you to understand it. But I attract that kind of trouble the way a lightning rod attracts lightning. Welly and Heather would agree, I think."

The two looked unhappy, but reluctantly nodded their heads.

Earl continued. "So I really have to go. It would be best to leave now, tonight." The others looked startled. "But I'll wait until morning. I think it might be best if Heather and Welly did not come with me, but I'll leave that to them."

"Of course we're coming with you," Heather protested, twisting a braid.

"Certainly. We have to," Welly added.

"No, you don't have to! It would be a good deal safer if you didn't. But you make your own decisions." Abruptly he excused himself to go pack his rucksack.

Breakfast was not a happy meal. Earl was brooding and silent, and Mrs. Penrose seemed on the verge of tears. Heather felt she was tearing down the middle; and looking at Welly, she knew he felt the same. Only John Wesley seemed unaffected, chattering about what he'd do the next time any sneaky old birdcat came their way.

Mrs. Penrose substituted several of the children's old, frayed blankets for warm ones of her own making, and she stuffed food in every cranny the three packs provided. Finally, the three stood outside the farmhouse door, coats on, hoods pulled up, and packs once again on their backs.

After Mrs. Penrose had kissed them all and lavished them with tearful good-byes, Earl pulled his hand from a pocket and extended it to her.

"This isn't payment. There's no way to repay your kindness. But it is beautiful."

He rolled onto her palm a large opal, the size of a pigeon egg. Holding the stone to the morning light, she gasped. It was alive with fire and color, as though all the world's sunsets were captured in its depths.

John Wesley jumped to see, and his mother brought it down to him. "Oh, that's the prettiest thing in the world!"

"I hope you enjoy it," Earl said, tousling the boy's hair. "Just don't play marbles with it and lose it down a rat hole. Your folks might enjoy it, too."

Together the three children walked out the farmyard gate. They stopped several times to wave, the last as the road topped a hill. The farm seemed small and safe in its little valley. The three Penroses stood at the door waving.

As they dropped down the crest, Heather whispered, "Perhaps we'll come back someday." Welly swallowed and nodded, but Earl strode ahead saying nothing.

Snow had fallen during the night, dusting the world in fresh whiteness. The road wound through it, a smooth ribbon of white on white, making its way south to the old coast. They had walked in silence for several miles when suddenly Earl stopped and turned back to them.

"No, it's no good. I can't let you come with me."

"What!" Welly exclaimed.

"I'm putting you in too much danger. What I said to the Penroses goes for you, too. Where I am, there's danger. And I haven't the power to protect you."

"But that creature . . ." Heather began.

"That creature was no common mutation. I don't know if

Morgan sent it, but it's odd she's left us along this long. It's been a wonderful respite, and I almost fooled myself into thinking it would last. But she'll never rest until she destroys me and anyone helping me."

"But, Earl," Heather protested, "we have to go with you."

"You do not! I've been too cowardly and self-centered to say that. Long ago, you discharged any obligation you had to me. It's I who've an obligation to you, to keep you safe. I said last night the decision was yours. But it's not. I knew the decision I had to make, and I didn't want to make it! Go back, go back to the Penroses. I'm sorry I've dragged you so far from your homes. But they'll be good to you. If I find Arthur—when I find Arthur—I'll try to come back."

"We can't leave you," Heather shouted. "You need us to—"

"I don't need you!" His voice was high and frantic. "I don't need you; I don't need anybody! I have to be alone—always!"

Grabbing their shoulders, he spun them around and shoved them back up the road. They stumbled ahead a few steps, then stopped. Heather stamped her foot angrily and turned back. "Earl, that's not—"

She fell silent. There was no one to be seen.

Her shock exploded into anger. "So who cares?" she shouted. "Who cares if you don't need us? The Penroses do! They have a place for us. Go on and be alone!"

The only answer was a vast silence and the whisper of drifting snow.

"What now?" Welly whispered. "Do we really turn back?"

Heather was shaking with misery. "I thought that's what I wanted. But I also thought he needed me, needed us. Maybe the Penroses really do. I don't know. What else is there?"

She turned and walked slowly up the road. Welly

followed. They trudged on, heads bowed, silent as the wilderness around them.

Finally Heather stopped and raised her head. "I'm so confused. Maybe we ought . . ."

A dark figure stood on the road ahead. Morgan.

THROUGH
THE FURNACE

THE WOMAN HAD AN AGELESS BEAUTY. RAVEN BLACK HAIR flowed free from her hood, framing a pale face and eyes of emerald green. She smiled sadly.

"So, he left you. That's like him. Always thinking first of himself and his own mad plans."

"No," Heather asserted. "He wanted to protect us."

"He didn't want you tagging along and being a bother. But that's his way, always using people for his own ends."

"That's not fair!" Welly protested.

"Fair? Has he been fair to you? He dragged you away from your home, your schooling. He subjected you to discomfort and dangers, most of which you couldn't understand. Think about it, have you ever been so miserable in your lives? Cold and wet, not enough food or sleep, always afraid?"

Heather shook her head slowly. "He didn't mean to—"

"He meant to use you. You were helpful in escaping from Llandoylan, in carrying provisions. You kept him company and amused him. But he's through with you now; you're becoming a hindrance. So he's left you alone in the middle of nowhere, hundreds of miles from home."

Heather stamped her foot, angry at herself as much as Morgan. "No! That's not true! None of it is! What he wants is right, it's good. When he finds—" She stopped short.

"Finds Arthur?" Morgan smiled at Heather's horror. "Don't fret. You haven't let out any secrets. I knew that must be his idea. He has a fixation about it, you know. But Arthur's dead. He died in battle two thousand years ago. His bones are dust, like the rest of Merlin's dreams."

"But he . . ." Welly began.

Morgan looked down at him, her green eyes wide with sympathy. "It's sad, really. Arthur was Merlin's life. He can't accept a world without him. He wasn't there that day to see him die, so now he grasps at fairy tales. It's a sick, mad obsession, and he'll probably follow it to the end of his days. But he shouldn't drag others with him."

The two children stood silent and confused.

Morgan extended her hands toward them. "Come. I never abandon friends in the wilderness. You have a place with me."

They pulled back. "No!"

"Come now. You followed him because you wanted adventure, to be part of something grand. You've had danger and hardship, but hardly adventure. Come with me and belong to a noble adventure! Oh, no doubt Merlin's filled you with lies about my evil powers. Certainly, I have power, but power can be used for good! Look at this wreck of a world. Look at the chaos, the stupidity! What is needed is order and direction. I can give it that." She smiled, stepping toward them. "You two are of this world's elite. Together we have the knowledge to remake this world, to overcome petty objections of the ignorant. And if you join with me, you can share this power. You can be as you want to be, as you are inside. And all the world will see you like that."

She reached out and took their hands. "Come, let me show you what you can be."

Heather looked into Morgan's green eyes, deeply into those eyes, and saw there her own reflection. It was her, it was Heather McKenna. But there was a difference. It was the real her: she was beautiful. Her hair was soft and thick and flowed about her shoulders, the pale blonde of winter sun. And her eyes were the ice blue of a rare bright sky.

She moved among crowds, and people parted for her, murmuring admiration. She mounted marble steps, and her gown swirled around her, the sparkling radiance of sunlight glittering on snow. As she climbed, it flowed into shadowy folds of deep, cold blue.

She reached the top and sat regally on a chair of stone. The world assembled in awe about her. Surely anyone with her beauty would be given whatever she wanted. But what was it she wanted? Oh yes, animals. She had liked animals: deer and squirrel, insects, lambs and birds. Let them come up. They hesitated, milling about. Animals love her. They will come up to her! How can she go down to them, someone of her beauty, her cool beauty? They need her, they love her. Let them come and show it.

They won't come. They don't need her beauty? They won't give the love due her beauty? Then let them wallow, the stupid beasts. She didn't need them. She had gifts enough. Gifts, yes; she had a gift. She raised her hand for all to see. The jewel flashed purple in her ring.

See, a gift! A gift given for her beauty. No, no for something else, something when she had no beauty. Given for . . . friendship. A friend gave her the purple jewel, a gift given for her friendship. A gift for a gift, that was right. Her gift, her ring, was to make things right. It had a charm to make things right.

She wanted things to be right. They were not right now.

They were wrong. She was not beautiful; she did not need to be. She had love and gave love. She needed friendship; and her friendship was needed. Things should be right, her gift made things right. She clutched the ring and its purple stone—purple like her poor friend's fuddled magic. Her friend who needed her. The magic, the charm made things right, all cracker jack. Cracker Jack!

The dais cracked, and the marble stairs crumbled. She fell down into purple, into warmth. She was loved, and she loved. Needed and was needed. And she was free.

Morgan smiled as she took Welly's hand and led him up a green hill. He bounded up easily because he was strong and lithe. He mounted his horse, his tall warhorse; his glasses fell away and shattered, yet he could see!

And below him he saw the plain of battle. He had made the battle plan and made it for himself. He would lead; all the troops below knew how clever was his plan and how brave his leadership, and they cheered and cheered him.

The clash of battle rose from below. His cunning ambush had come about; the battle cry went up, and they shouted his name. Muscular legs planted firmly apart, he called out bold instructions. The slaughter was great, and he exulted in it.

Now the enemy broke through and rushed upon his height. He had no fear. Pulling out his great sword, he beat them back. Nigel and Justin and the other taunters, they shrank back and cried out. The great dukeling cringed before him, and Welly took his sword and plunged it into his body.

The blood spurted red, and Nigel's face crumpled in pain. The boy's friends wailed around him as he lay small and sad upon the ground, and a girl held his broken body and rocked back and forth, back and forth—as another girl had rocked, with another dead thing. She had been his friend, that other girl, and he had fought to help her, as another friend had fought to help him.

All below him now wailed in sadness and loss; his troops and the others, the same. He looked down at their pain and agony, and they called out against the misery he'd brought. They cried against his clever plans. He saw them over the head of his horse. His warhorse, his knight's horse. White and smooth, its neck was arched and its ears pricked forward and pricked his fingers also as he clutched at it in his pocket. His knight, from his friend. He was his friend's knight, his friend who fought for him and knighted him and needed him. His friends needed him. And someone called to him. Called that it would be all right. All right! All Cracker Jack!

The call beat on him, blew at him, swept away the sound of battle. Swept him away, far away. And free.

Masked in invisibility, Earl hurried down the road, ignoring his friends' calls. Every step hurt. But it was hurt himself or hurt them. He had made the choice.

Miles passed as he marched doggedly, fixed on his goal. On his longer legs he moved faster without his companions. It gave him no pleasure. He strove to keep his mind blank, set only on moving forward. But thoughts kept nibbling at the edges, intruding into the blankness.

He was running. Running from the farm, running from his friends. Running because he could not protect them, protect them from the danger he brought them.

But what was he running to? He had a quest, a mission. Yet so far he had failed. Would it be any different with Arthur? Could he protect him, when he surely would be in far greater danger? Could he be of any real aid to Arthur in the tasks before him in this shattered world?

He stopped abruptly in the middle of the road. Was he of any use to anybody? Even to himself, if he dared not keep simple friendships?

Slowly he walked off the road, noting for the first time that snow was falling. The wind was up, sweeping an empty, mournful howl through the wilderness. He knew what he must do.

Earl stood in the snow and looked into its spinning whiteness. He let his pack slip from his back. Slowly he took off his coat and cast it away from him, and his jacket and gloves. He would either become one with this world and learn its rhythms, or he would die in it.

He spread his arms, reaching into the sky, and shouted with his mind, "World of my cold and blasted future, I will be one with you! Either as part of your living pulse, your waves of power and life, or dead as your frozen dust. I will be yours. Take me now!"

He looked up into the swirling snow as he had that day when he'd sought only escape, not knowing the danger of what he did, of losing himself forever. Now he knew. The snow fell lazily from the sky, big, soft flakes spinning down toward him. He willed to be one with them, those flakes that swirled down at him, up at him, around with him. His soul thinned into them. He was snow, swirling with snow, swirling on the wind.

Bodiless, he blew on the wind. Blew over the world, blew over the rocks, rasping against their hardness, blew through the trees, jangling their needles with music. He blew through the thatch of houses and churned the smoke of their fires. He blew over the ocean, caressing the water into billowy waves and whipping the crests with foam. He blew high into the sky above the seas and land. He tore at the clouds, shredding them and seeing beyond.

Beyond were the stars, calling in their splendid beauty. He rose up toward them through eternal emptiness, through endless silence. They glowed with the brightness of beginnings.

Yet embers still glowed on the earth behind him. It pulsed with warmth that pulled at him. Pulled him back, back through emptiness; pulled him deep, deep into its core. Its throbbing heat rose outward. It rose up through the rock;

through heavy, patient rock that had known only itself, and higher stone with sunken memories of the sky.

The pulse of warmth rose to the crumbling surface, to the rich soil. Roots sank into it and drained out warmth and life. Plants raised their heads to the sky, bowing in the wind, weighed by the snow, giving nourishment and shelter to life that huddled among them or bounded over them.

The web closed, the patterns settled into place. The swirling snow and empty wind, the pulsing stars, the answering throbs in stone and the upward surging of life. All were tied in glowing traceries, in interlocking spheres. The web of force and power and rightness was part of all creation and part of him. Part of his cells and consciousness and joy.

Heather opened her eyes. She was lying on her side on an empty road. Snow sifted silently from the sky. A hand rested in hers. She recoiled, but it was not Morgan's hand; it was Welly's. She squeezed it.

He opened his eyes with a befuddled smile. "Is it all right, then? For both of us?"

"Yes. Yes, I think it is." She looked down at her hand and its glinting purple ring. "But it may not be for him. That was all rot, you know, about his not needing us. He's just a confused kid like the rest of us." She smiled. "He needs me. I know that now. And you, too."

"Maybe. But not as his general."

"As his friend, then."

"Yes, as his friend." He stood up, surveying the white, swirling landscape. "But how do we find him, when we can't even see him?"

"He won't stay invisible forever. Down this road someone's bound to have seen him. We'll find him. We have to."

They started down the southern road, snow slicing across their path in icy blasts. They staggered on against it until the darkness of the storm shaded into the darkness of night.

Dizzy with exhaustion, they took shelter behind a rocky outcrop and slipped into dream-washed sleep.

In the morning, the snow lay deep and quiet about them, but the sky was hazily clear. A smear of orange spread upward from the east. Hastily sharing some bread, the two children donned their packs and stepped from their rocky shelter.

They started back to the road and stopped abruptly. Lying half-buried in the snow, some thirty feet away, was a body. Beside it lay a discarded pack, coat and jacket.

Heather and Welly ran fearfully toward it, then slowed. The sun, just rising in the east, seemed to catch and play along a web of light, a faint intricate tracery that enclosed the snowcovered body. Then the sun cleared the horizon, and the pattern faded.

They hurried to him and dropped to their knees. Heather brushed the snow from his face. "Oh, Earl," she moaned and clutched at his hand. It was cold as death. His face was serene and pale as the snow.

The eyelids fluttered, disturbing their fringing of ice. Slowly Earl opened his eyes. "It's all right, then?" he whispered, his voice barely audible.

"Yes, all right," Heather sobbed in joy. "It's all, all right."

thirteen

BATTLE ON THE TOR

TOGETHER THEY HELPED EARL STAND, AND RETRIEVING HIS things, they led him back to their shelter of the night. Stiffly he pulled on jacket and coat and sat down on a rock. With an easy movement of his hand, he started a fire blazing on the surface of the snow. In minutes, life and warmth were surging through his body.

He spoke little of what had transpired. He was again in touch with his power, again in harmony with his world and its forces. That was enough for him to share. But he was interested in the halting accounts of the other's ordeals.

When they'd finished, he sighed. "Once Morgan tapped my weakness and ensnared me in it. And I didn't see until too late. I, a wily old wizard! But you saw her trap and broke it. I'm impressed."

"We had help," Heather said softly.

"The only help you had was in yourselves, and what your friendship gave those tokens."

Earl stood up and stretched, feeling every fiber of his being tingling and alive. He extinguished his magic flame with a word. "We've all been through the furnace, it seems. Now, lets see how well we're forged."

They shouldered their packs and set off together. Before long, Earl led them from the road, striking across country to the southwest. "Have you a better idea where we're heading?" Welly asked.

"Not really. But I'm more certain that there *is* someplace worth heading for."

The snow-blanketed fields dropped into a long valley. Down its length ran a dull silver ribbon that flashed back sunlight like the blade of a sword.

"The River Tamar," Earl announced. "The boundary that divides Devon from Cornwall."

The river was frozen into stillness. They found its valley strewn with debris from summer floods. Heading for the river, they picked their way through bits of tree and brush, rocks and the occasional scrap of human handiwork. Earl moved more slowly, looking thoughtfully about him. Then he cut off on a tangent across the valley floor until, exclaiming with satisfaction, he bent down and examined something.

Welly and Heather followed to see what he'd discovered and found him kneeling by a young uprooted pine, a few brittle needles still clinging to its boughs. Pulling out his sword, Earl began hacking off the branches. The others squatted down and watched, figuring they'd get an explanation in time. At last, he seemed satisfied. The slender trunk, bare of branches and bark, shone a soft yellow. At one end there remained a gnarled claw where the roots had begun.

Jabbing the thin end into the ground, he declared, "There, a first class staff."

Welly looked dubiously toward the slope on the far side of the valley. "It doesn't look all that steep to me."

Earl flashed him a look of theatrical scorn. "A wizard's staff!" he said with mock thunder, tossing his work from hand to hand testing its weight. "I was afraid to use one earlier. It helps concentrate power, and the sort of magic I was producing didn't bear concentration."

Heather smiled mischievously. "You mean we might have had a forty-foot-high purple pie?"

Earl laughed. "Something like."

They walked to the edge of the frozen river. Standing on the bank, Earl tapped the surface firmly with his staff. "The Tamar's a lot narrow here than the Severn where we crossed it. This should be frozen enough to walk on."

Welly and Heather followed him cautiously onto the ice. Its surface had been roughened by the wind, but still produced a good slide. In moments, the two were executing glides, swoops and occasional spills on the frozen river. Earl joined them, using his staff to vault into acrobatics, sometimes ending in a spinning sprawl of arms, staff and long legs. The valley echoed to whoops and gleeful yells, until at last the three collapsed exhausted on the western bank.

Heather looked at Earl and giggled. "I guess you were right. You're definitely a fourteen-year-old, outside and in."

Laughing, he flopped over in the snow and looked at her. "And you were right, too. There're some very good things about a teenager."

Awkwardly he placed a hand on hers. "And I've learned some other things. There are mistakes I won't make again. I won't deny that I need people."

She smiled shyly. "And I won't deny that I need to be needed."

Rested finally, the three climbed the opposite side of the valley. Once on the level again, Earl pointed to a dark table-like rise in the south. "Our route takes us by that tor. It's not the goal; I think that lies beyond. But it's an interesting spot none the less."

"It's a queer-shaped hill, all right." Welly said.

"It's an old Iron Age hill fort," Earl replied. "Pre-Roman, but when I knew it, the fortifications were still well intact. I imagine it's weathered a bit since."

Welly was interested now. "I've read about them. Aren't they surrounded by banks and ditches?"

Earl nodded. "Most of the people lived outside the forts, but when enemies threatened, they and their livestock moved behind the walls. They have views in all directions. Very defensible. See a lone, flat-topped hill anywhere in Britian, and you've probably fround an Iron Age hill fort."

Throughout the day, they trudged on toward the tor. Having a fixed goal that drew closer gave a feeling of achievement. But as sunset neared, they still seemed uncomfortably distant. Earl had been feeling more and more uneasy as the afternoon worn on, on now he urged them to greater speed.

"We know Morgan's about, but that in itself doesn't bother me. She may be content just to watch us. But there are other things, evil, distorted things. I feel them. And her long absence worries me. She was up to something, and it may not bode us any good."

"What you're saying," Welly said, panting, "is that we'd better get to that hill fort before nightfall."

"Exactly."

Night was indeed falling when they reached the tor and began scrambling up its steep side. The sky had been unusually clear all day, and now the full moon shone through a high, thin curtain. As they walked, rocks and humps in the snow cast deep black shadows in the silvery light.

At last they reached the top and passed through breaks in the embankments that encircled the crown of the hill. Not long before the Devastation, restorers had cleared the ditch and rebuilt the walls. But there were still major gaps and sagging spots, the work of both time and seekers after building stone.

Still, any walls gave the travelers some feeling of security. Choosing a sturdy section to break the west wind, they gratefully took off their packs and brought out some food. Earl ignited a small domestic fire while Welly rigged up a blanket lean-to against the wall. The bank of clouds along the western horizon suggested they might be due for a storm.

They dined on bread and strips of dried meat, but throughout the meal Earl kept getting up and walking to the opposite wall to look east. Again and again they hazy moonlight showed only an empty landscape. But this didn't shake his conviction that something was coming.

At last he saw it. A blackness appeared in the east that was not a cloud. It spread inklike over the plain, and the moonlight did not penetrate it. Slowly it rolled toward their hill.

Noting his suddenly rigid attention, the other two joined him. "What is it?" Heather asked quietly.

"An army of sorts. Morgan's army."

With growing alarm, they watched the advance. This, Welly realized, might be the eve of his first battle. But he feared he wasn't feeling the appropriate sentiments of a warrior. Heroes always seemed exultant, eager for the fray. He felt cold and weak. But he would stick it out. And if it proved to be his last battle as well as his first, at least he'd be spared this wait again.

The black wave flowed closer, lapping around the base of the hill. The moonlight and the glow of their own green torches made the enemy visible. Too visible.

"Well, now we know where Morgan spent last month," Earl said bitterly. "On a recruiting drive among the east coast invaders." The mutant creatures below were men and beasts and horrible blendings. Most, Earl imagined, were twisted in mind as well as in body: easy conquests for Morgan, ready to hear a voice like hers and follow. He flinched at the thought of what their progress had been like: a steady ravaging of land, which had little left to ravage.

Standing on the ancient earthen battlements, he scanned the crowd below. His eyes and other senses picked out creatures from a world more distorted even than devastated Europe. They reeked of unnatural evil; beings alien to this world and eager to taste its blood.

Sounds drifted from below. Howls and yapping, inhuman laughter and shrieks. Earl left the others and, chanting words under his breath, walked around the wall's perimeter, moving his hand in quick, decisive gestures.

Now the sounds rose in intensity. From out of the dark, roiling crowd moved a figure edged in fiery green. Morgan's black hair and cape blew wildly about her. At her side strode a huge gray wolf, and she rode a beast like the one at the Penrose farm, yet far larger. Its whiplike tail was split in two, and the mane surrounding its cruel face was longer and seemed tipped with fire. Strange ridges ran down its side, suggesting folded wings. And it cry was terrible.

When its unearthly screech had ceased ringing from the sky, Morgan called out Merlin's name.

Earl stepped up on the wall, his voice rolling down in derisive waves. "Morgan, are you and your friends going somewhere? If so, I suggest you save yourself a climb. This hill just goes down again on the other side."

"Little boy, don't joke with me!" she screamed in reply. "I give you one last chance to join me."

"Join with your netherworld friends and all this world's sweepings? No thank you, Morgan. I choose my own companions."

"Children and dreamers; some companions! You are a fool, Merlin. In every age, you are a fool. And you deserve to live in none!"

She shrieked a command, and the creatures about her answered in deafening response. Like a loosed flood, they surged up the base of the hill. A frontal attack, Welly thought, with an attempt at detachment. Very unsophisticated. But with the numbers balanced as they were, he feared that sophistication was less than essential.

He and Heather stood close together, gazing at the approaching hoard. But Earl paid it scant attention. Standing alone on the inner wall, he bent low, swinging his staff in a flat arch and snapping out orders.

At the base of the outer bank, a line of purple sparks appeared. Quickly they grew into tall columns of flame. Swaying back and forth like huge snakes, the flames broke loose and began weaving down the slope toward the oncoming army. Some in that force quailed at the sight and ran off into the night. Others held their ground, but shrieked when the pillars of fire coiled into their midst. Many were consumed.

Over the land the night wind was rising. Suddenly the three on the hilltop were hit from behind by powerful gusts. The storm that had lurked in the west had crept up behind them. With a deep rumble of thunder, the dark clouds cracked open, and rain cascaded from the sky. The columns of battling flames hissed furiously and sputtered out.

A flash of lightning froze the scene before them, showing the dark forces in a new advance. They were led now by a pack of long, skeletal creatures, with huge eyes and translucent skins.

"They're coming!" Heather yelled over the crashing rain and thunder.

"Stand back from me!" Earl yelled in return. "When the next lightning come, keep clear!"

The sky split down the middle and spilled out blinding light. Earl stood with his legs braced apart and thrust up his arms as if reaching into the storm. Lightning jabbed down toward him. Suddenly it swerved and arched away to explode into mass advancing up the slope. The crash of thunder obscured all but the first screams, but not the smell of charred flesh and fur.

Morgan cried out. From the back of her rearing mount, she too reached toward the sky. She seemed to grab at a spear of lightning and send it hurtling off to where the three stood. Earl flung up an arm. The bolt veered aside, but smashed into the top of the hill, leaving a new smoldering gap in the walls.

A growling cheer rose from below, and the opponents that remained, again surged forward. "Still too many of them." Earl muttered. Head tilted, he surveyed their advance. Then crouching down, he spread his arms out wide.

In the ditch surrounding the fort, the air quivered and jelled into a lurid purple mist. It glowed coldly within itself. Pouring over the outer bank, it flowed down the slope, sweeping over the front ranks. From its shroud rose coughs and gasping cries.

A gust of wind from the east smashed into the cloud and pushed it back up the slope, to thin and vanish. But where it had lain, the ground was littered with dead or writhing bodies.

A lull descended over the battle. The storm was rolling off toward the north. It continued its sky-bound battle in the distance, one mountains cloud after another briefly rimming itself in light. It had been a natural storm, after all, Earl decided, not one of Morgan's making. But she had used it well.

The remaining creatures milled about on the slope. Some could be seen slipping to the fringes of the mob and slinking off over the plain. With threatening commands, Morgan urged her troops on. The huge wolf beside her leaped into their midst, tearing at the hesitant until its jaw dripped with blood. Again the attackers moved forward.

They were fewer now, but they were closer. Earl jumped

down from the wall into the fort, dropping to his knees by a rain puddle. Dredging both hands into it, he pulled up dripping handfuls of mud. Frantically he patted this sticky mass into a roughly human shape. Peeling a splinter from the base of his staff, he stuck it into the mannekin's crudely molded hand.

Cradling his creation in both hands, he climbed back onto the wall to see the formost of the attackers almost at the outer bank. Shouting a string of rasping words, he lifted his hands above his head and hurled the figure through the air. It shattered on the crest of the lower bank.

The fragments splattered over the hillside. Wherever one fell, it rapidly grew into a life-sized humanoid: larger, but as lumpy and misshapened as the first. And these new figures moved forward, each clutching a staff licked with purple flame.

Clumsily the creatures lurched down the hill. Wherever one encountered an enemy and swiped it with its fiery staff, the other screamed and burst into flame. But when an enemy struck first at a mud thing, the mannekin broke apart into lifeless shreds.

Watching from below, Morgan screamed in anger. She jerked back on the reins of her mount. It squealed with the sound of tearing steel. Rearing back, it spread great coppery wings. With mighty thrumming, the winds beat in the air, and together the creature and its rider rose into the night.

They lifted high above the battle, higher than the hilltop. With a laugh like the cry of night birds, Morgan raised one hand into the air and whirled it over her head. Out from her hand spun a sinuous light. It grew and crackled, and along its length rose a shivering curtain, pulsing and fading and glowing again, an aurora of shimmering greens.

With a flick of her wrist, Morgan sent the glowing serpent snapping toward them. From its tip, great bolts of green fire broke free and showered over the hilltop and into the fort. Whatever they hit burst into flame.

As the firebolts crashed around them, Welly and Heather huddled together, staring in awe at the flying apparition. But Earl, his gaunt face glistening with sweat, concentrated on his work. He drove the tip of his staff violently into the earth. As chanted, purple fire ran up its shaft and spread into tangled branches.

At a word, the limbs bloomed with flame. Wrenching the firetree from the ground, he held it aloft and shook it. Blossoms of purple flame broke loose, arching into the sky. Some smashed into oncoming green fireballs; others rained down among the attackers.

The night air raged with light, screams and the hiss of falling flames. Heather and Welly were tempted to drop to the ground and hurl protective arms over their heads. What kept them on their feet was a vision of hideous attackers somehow breaking through and jumping on their backs.

They looked nervously about the broken circle of earth and saw that indeed some creatures had made it through. Urgently the two turned to Earl. Lean and pale in the eerie light, he stood on the bank above them swinging his flaming tree. The wind whipped his hair wildly about his face, and all his senses were focused on the battle overhead, meeting volley with volley. Their eyes met, and the two children closed in behind him, holding up their bright Eldritch swords.

The gleaming blades seemed to know swordsmanship, as their wielders did not, and the two thrust and parried with startling effectiveness. Dark blood sprayed the air. Several attackers drew back and disappeared into the night.

A slimy gray creature singled out Heather. Its cold-eyed reptilian head rose from a tangle of tentaclelike arms. It hissed venomously as one arm swiftly coiled up and wrapped around her throat. The thing was cold and slick. Its surface rippled as muscles constricted around her windpipe. With one hand she scrabbled feebly at the tightening coil, while her other arm awkwardly brought up the sword. Several desperate slices and she severed the tentacle. The strangling segment loosened and slithered lifelessly to the ground—as she gasped for breath. Undaunted, the creature sent forth two more arms to entangle her weapon, but she leaped back and hacked wildly into the writhing mass.

Welly confronted a squat, goblin-creature, each of its three hairy arms wielding a club. The thing was clumsy but powerful. The flashing sword splintered of the clubs, but another broke through the blade's defense and smashed jarringly into Welly's right shoulder. The whole arm went numb. His deadened fingers dropped the sword into his other hand. Wielded left-handed, the sword moved awkwardly, but it came from an unexpected angle and took the slow-witted creature by surprise. With a looping swing, Welly sliced off one of its ears. In an arc of blood, the ear sailed into the darkness, and with a gurgling whine its former owner followed it.

Welly paused to fight down sickness, then shakily he turned to help Heather. But his eye caught the flicker of something gray rocketing up the hillside. Welly's skin prickled as he watched the thing dart from one concealing shadow to another. It was the huge wolf they had seen at Morgan's side.

Worse that anything from his fevered nightmares, it was three times larger than a fell-dog. And where those creatures had merely been hungry, this beast seemed afire with evil. It slunk on its belly through a still-smoldering gap in the wall. Its hair was brindled and gray, its yellow eyes wicked and close set. The tongue flicked snakelike between yellowed fangs. And, before it, there flowed a wave of cold.

The thing stood in a shadow of crumbling wall and

looked cooly about the shattered fort and at its three defenders. The jaw dropped open, and there came a low growling laugh.

Hunching down, it began stalking toward Earl, whose whole attention was fixed on the fiery clash with Morgan. Twenty feet from its prey, the creature jumped onto a large rock.

Welly crouched in the shadow of the bank. Numbing cold flowed about him as it had on another night. His hair bristled at the memory, and his hands grew slick and clammy. But slowly he stood up and, stepping out from the shadow, raised his sword between Earl and the huge wolf. The beast glanced down at him, an evil intelligence flickering in its eyes. Then, ears pricked forward, it raised its head and surveyed its goal and the gap between them.

Deliberately the beast crouched down, great muscles bunching and rippling under its fur. A growl rose form deep in its chest. Suddenly it sprang into the air, arching high over Welly's head. Welly yelled and leaped straight upward. His sword point gouged the beast down the length of its belly.

The creature spun sideways and crashed onto the ground. Snarling, it rolled over in mud already bloodied from its long wound. It crouched to spring again. Without pausing, Welly hurled himself at it, thrusting his blade deep into the shaggy chest. The wolf jerked violently and threw back its head. Its howl shattered the night.

The body shuddered, pulled away from Welly's now-smoking blade and lay still. Its coarse wolf features slowly blurred and changed into those of a man. Garth.

At that dying howl, silence fell like ice over the battle. Earl spun around to see what was happening behind him. "I should have guessed," he said as even the human form dissolved into dust. "Morgan's consort was a werewolf."

Welly looked down at the smoldering mud where the

body had lain. This was his first kill in battle, and it was not the grand thing he'd imagined, even with a victim as foul as this. He felt oddly weak and polluted. Again, he wondered if he would be sick. It would be almost a relief.

Earl had turned back to the battle, but there was little left there. In his brief moments of inattention, Morgan and her mount had vanished. Their snaking green aurora was already fading from the sky. Below, those attackers not dead on the hillside were fleeing in panic into the night. Weary of killing, he let them go.

Heather had dispatched her opponent by finally lopping off its reptilian head. Shaking with fatigue, she joined her companions. Her face was ashen, her thin hair plastered to her forehead with sweat.

The three surveyed the suddenly silent battlefield. It was now lit only by a mist-shrouded moon and by patches of fire, green and purple, that still glowed about the hillside. These burned with cold fuelless flame, except they fed on corpses.

Heather, her lips pale thin lines, asked weakly, "Is it all over? Is Morgan gone for good?"

Earl nodded wearily, leaning on his now flameless staff. "She's gone, though hardly for good. But this battle's over at least. I hope she's had her fill of direct confrontation. I certainly have."

He swayed where he stood. Alarmed, Welly caught him and kept him from falling.

"I'm all right," Earl said shakily. "I just need some rest. I can't handle this sort of thing so well anymore. I'm not as old as I used to be, you know."

They helped him over to their camp. The makeshift tent had burned, but most of their other equipment was only scorched.

Earl sank into the blankets they pulled out for him, and in moments he was asleep. Wrapping themselves in their own blankets, Welly and Heather lay down at the base of the wall. Their minds buzzed with sounds and images, but they were too tired to talk or sort anything out. They felt no need to set watch. There was not the slightest whiff of menace in the air. Exhausted, they drifted into the night's numbing calm.

❈ f o u r t e e n ❈

ON MAGIC'S SHORE

HEATHER'S DREAMS FADED INTO MORNING MIST. SHE REmained curled in her blanket, eyes closed, trying to remember where in their long trek they had camped the night before. She remembered, and her eyes flew open.

The sun was already well up. From beside her, where Welly had bedded down, came the sound of slow, steady breathing. Then she heard another sound and stiffened. Somewhere to her left there was a quiet snuffling.

Images swirled back of the nightmare creatures that had swarmed here the night before. She slipped a hand from her blankets and poked Welly. He snorted and rolled over.

"Hush," she whispered. "There's something over there."

His bleary eyes peered from the blankets, and a plump hand crept out, fumbled for his glasses and thrust them on his face. Slowly they both sat up and looked toward the center of the ruined hill fort. What they saw was definitely a mutant, but not the sort to inspire fear.

In the weak morning light, its thick coat glowed a snowy white. Its face and long legs were slender, like a deer's, but it was shaggy as a wild goat and its tail was long and horselike. Its two horns were separate for only a short distance. Then they became entwined and for several inches twisted together into a single point.

Heather glanced toward Earl's place and saw that he too was awake and watching the creature. A bemused smile lit his face.

The animal continued browsing at the grass, which the battle's heat had cleared the snow. Gradually it moved away. Cocking its ears, it suddenly raised its head and looked toward them, its large eyes soft and luminous. The animal and children watched each other for a moment, then it turned and, with a graceful bound, leaped over the bank and was gone.

Earl sighed and sat up. "Mythical or extinct, they seem to have made a comeback. And look at this." Cautiously he fingered some thorny brambles where, in the dark of the night, they had spread his blankets. Nestled among pointed leaves were several tiny pink buds.

"Wild roses," he said softly. "Remember the inn, The Rose and Unicorn? And I thought they were both hopelessly things of the past!" He laughed and climbed out of his blankets. "Mabe there's hope for this battered world yet!"

Over breakfast of bread and cheese, Earl said to the others, "Before I folded up last night, I should have thanked you. Wizard or not, without rear guard I wouldn't have made it. It was a ghastly thing for you to be subjected to. But . . . I needed you there."

Heather smiled. "Can't say I'd volunteer for that sort of duty every night. But I guess we make a good team."

"We do indeed."

Welly, blushing with pleasure, cleared his throat, "So where to now, Captain?"

In answer Earl stood up, and they followed him to the fort's south rim. He pointed over the earthen bank to the ocean and both coasts, the new and old. "We're headed there somewhere."

Heather stared at the ocean excitedly. The she frowned. "Do you think Morgan will leave us alone that long?"

Earl nodded. "She called in reinforcements last night and failed. I suspect she'll bide her time now and watch where we're going. When we're close enough to learn that ourselves, we may hear from her again."

They descended the south side of the hill, where the night's battle was less evident than on the eastern slope. But even so, the grass still smoldered in black patches, and the air smelled heavily of burning and death. They skirted twisted half-burned bodies. Brief, quickly averted glances showed hideous inhuman forms, made more hideous by death. Furred scavengers already skulked over the hillside.

The starkness of the battlefield brought a new vision of the battle itself. Then it had been too quick, too appalling and fantastic to be totally believable. Now the reality sank in. They walked largely in silence for the rest of the morning.

By midafternoon they'd sighted a small village and decided to stop for supplies. Veering west, they picked up a rutted track, which led to the small town square. On every side, stone houses huddled together under heavy turf roofs, and in the center rose a time-battered stone cross. Around it several merchants had set up booths, which were doing a livelier business in gossip than in trade. The sight of children traveling alone with coins for provisions caused only minor comment, for interest was centered on events the locals had witnessed the night before.

Lights had been seen in the northern sky, and outlying farmers near the tor reported weird happenings. Reports of flying monsters were generally discounted. But persistent sightings of other strange creatures throughout the area could not be dismissed, particularly when accompanied by the bloody slaughter of sheep, cattle and, in one case, a shepherd.

When it was learned that the three young strangers had come from the north, all attention swiveled to them.

"So, lad," a leatherworker asked Earl, "what did you see? I'd say you're lucky to have passed through that country alive, judging by what I've heard."

The others in the crowd muttered in agreement and waited for the boy's reply.

"Well, we . . . er . . . didn't see all that much worth talking about. We were camped and slept most of the night, I guess. There were lights by the tor, but then there was a storm, so it could have been lightning or something."

"Didn't you see any strange beasts?" a woman asked incredulously. "Why, my Sam, he saw two this morning!"

Earl squirmed, recalling the dregs of Morgan's forces spreading in panic over the plains. "Yes, there were creatures, very evil looking things. I think you'd all be wise to stay close to home the next few days and pen up your livestock."

This set off debate over the merits of taking some action, and the three children tried to slip away. But they were riveted by the comments of one gray-bearded farmer.

"If you ask me, it smacks of magic," he said, nodding. "Strong magical doings were going on at the tor last night, count on it. The days of magic are returning to this world. Blast me, if they aren't."

"What makes you think that, old man?" Earl asked quietly.

"Why it makes sense, don't it? There used to be magic in the old, old days, didn't there? Stories say so, before people learned how to do all that nonsense with science. Well, science took over, but did no good in the end, did it? What's going to work now? What's going to hold this old world together except magic, I'd like to know. Makes sense that does."

"Oh, come on, Will," joshed one of the younger men. "You'll be giving these kids worse nightmares then they'll have had already. You're always going on about magic and portents. You'd think we were living in some fairy-tale age.''

"Well, maybe we are,'' the old man muttered as he shuffled away, shaking his head, "or soon will be. Maybe indeed.''

With refilled packs, the three children slipped out of the village, leaving it to its rumors and speculations. Welly and Heather walked with lifted spirits. Strangers confirming what they'd seen made them feel more comfortably normal. Earl was silent, thinking about old Will and his faith in magic and portents. He suspected the old man sensed a truth. The cycles of this world were changing. A time of magic was beginning again.

That evening they stopped at a farmhouse. The family had been reluctant to open the door, with all the rumors of strange creatures abroad. But when they saw it was only children, they willingly offered their barn. They might have offered a place by their fire, had the children tried looking pathetic. But none of the three felt up to socializing.

In the morning, the fresh salt tang of the air spoke of the sea. Before long, they crossed the broken pavement of the old coast road and stood on bluffs overlooking what had once been a narrow wave-washed beach.

Now a sandy rock-strewn plain stretched out and down toward a distant expanse of water. Overhead, a rare sea gull cried shrilly and sailed seaward. Heather tingled with excitement, and even Welly was impressed with the size and power of the ocean, viewed at a safe distance.

To the east, the cliffs curved out in a long arm that eventually reached and jutted into the receded waters. Head tilted, Earl stood surveying this and the rest of the scene: the flat, dark horizon, the white fringe of breakers along the now-distant beach, the wrinkled gray surface of the sea dotted with occasional rocks and islands.

He sighed with mingled satisfaction and sadness. "It's a

new landscape for me, but I think I know where we're going now."

"Where?" the others asked together.

Earl glanced uneasily around and shook his head. "Let's just go there."

They searched several minutes for a way down the cliffs, at last finding traces of a path used of old by picnickers and bathers. Once on the ancient beach, Heather and Welly were soon running over the sand, leaping rocks and exclaiming over the occasional weathered shell.

Earl walked more quietly. Nostalgia and regret blew at him like the salt wind. Both whipped his eyes with tears. That descendants of his people should smash their civilization was perhaps their own affair. But that they should maim even its ageless oceans, that seemed a great deal to forgive.

Only a thin veil of snow covered the sand; the sea breezes swept most of it back against the cliffs. The air was cold and tangy with the scent of ocean.

As they neared the new shoreline, Heather was delighted with the rolling gray-green waters and the luminous curl of the breakers before they crashed into foam and surged up the sand. Welly, recalling Morgan's frightful illusion, was more reserved.

While the two younger children played keep-away with the farthest-reaching waves, Earl set about gathering flotsom from the beach. After half an hour, he'd made a pile of driftwood, seaweed, a few bird feathers and the jagged neck of an ancient bottle. He looked at it with dissatisfaction and called to the others.

"Hey, you two, come and help me or this'll take all day. The oceans don't wash up as much junk as they used to. Less wood to drift, I guess. There're not even many shells."

The two trotted back over the wave-smoothed sand, faces flushed and damp with spray. "Well, give us a clue," Welly said. "What are you up to?"

"I'm going to build a boat," he said simply. "If I ever get enough materials."

The others looked quizzically at the odds and ends piled at his feet. "With that?" Heather asked.

"To start with, yes. If we can get enough natural materials, I'll cement them together into the right form."

The three spread out over the beach, collecting things. Earl had said to take anything, so Welly and Heather, scouting together, picked up slimy shreds of seaweed, a few shells, water-smoothed stones and an occasional piece of wood, tossed and worn by the waves into bone-smooth whiteness.

In a shallow cove a quarter mile up the beach, they made a discovery. The bleached skeleton of some large sea animal had been washed high up on the beach. Scavengers had removed every vestige of meat, and the bones had finally tired and fallen away from each other. But most still remained scattered about the sand. Whent hey called Earl, he was excited. Gathering up an armload of broad, flat rib bones, he returned with them to his growing pile of junk.

At last he determined they had enough. The others sat on gritty, sand-dusted rocks as he spread his finds over the ground. At first they seemed no order in his work, but finally they made out the rough shape of a boat, its gunwales defined by curbing rib bones. Inside these, he arranged the other things, fitting them together like pieces in a jigsaw puzzle, until as little space as possible showed between them. The rocks he discarded, saying they had "too many sinking instincts to overcome."

At last he stood back and, head tilted, surveyed his work with satisfaction. Welly was less impressed. "If you think I'm going out to sea in that, you're dead wrong," he announced flatly.

Earl shot him a look of scorn. "This is just the first step, ye of little faith. Now we'll see about binding it together."

He dropped to his knees in the sand. Leaning over his

strange creation, he began passing his hands smoothly over the individual pieces, all the while muttering words in interweaving singsong. As his hands passed for the third or fourth time over some items, these seemed to blur, their edges to spread and blend into the objects around them.

Gradually the whole became a solid sheet, a flat boat-shaped cutout of splotchy gray. Then Earl changed the rhythm of his chant and began moving quickly around the edges, working them with his hands, pulling them up like a potter molding clay.

Finally, a boat rested before them on the sand, fifteen feet long, the shape and color of a fish. Its prow was high and gracefully upturned. Its stern, though broader, also rose above the tapered sides. Down its length ran a knife-edged keel.

Despite their doubts, the two children were impressed. Welly slid off his rock and walked over to Earl's creation. He touched it cautiously, as though expecting it to bite or fall apart. When it did neither, he stroked its smooth sides and even kicked it reservedly.

"Well," he admitted, "it feels real enough, and it looks like a boat. But it has one problem."

Earl frowned at his handiwork. "What?"

"It *is* a boat! I won't go floating out on all that water in any kind of boat, least of all one that's held together by words!"

"Welly, this is very trustworthy stuff. Magic-blended objects are stronger than illusions. They don't have to be tended all the time like creating-spells."

"Maybe so, but that doesn't change the fact that there's a lot of water out there, and I can't swim!"

"There's really not much water to cross. We haven't far to go now." Earl lowered his voice. "We're heading for that rock."

"Which, the big island?"

"No, the cluster of rocks to its left, the far one."

"And you're sure we have to go there?" Welly pressed.

"*I* have to go there. I'm sure the key to entering Avalon is there. You can stay behind, of course, but it will leave you unprotected, and Morgan may still be about."

Welly jumped slightly and looked suspiciously back at the cliffs and long, empty stretch of beach.

Heather spoke up. "Welly, I can't swim either, at least not much. But who knows what Earl's going to find once he gets there or what he'll have to do. He may need us. We've stuck together so far. I don't want to miss what happens next."

Welly kicked the sand at his feet. "Well, I don't, either. I'm coming, of course. It's just that I signed on to be a soldier, not a sailor. Water's not trustworthy."

The tide was rising closer to the completed boat. They loaded in their packs, and the three paddles that Earl had fashioned, two from larger pieces of driftwood and one from his own staff. Then, with Earl on one side and Welly and Heather on the other, they lifted the boat, finding it surprisingly light, and ran down to the in-rolling waves.

When knee-deep in the cold, foamy water, Earl ordered them to jump in: Heather in front, Welly in the middle. Earl, himself took the steering position at the stern. Quickly they grabbed up paddles and dug into the foam. Pulled by undertow and pushed by incoming surges, they moved out swiftly, their propulsion magically enhanced. They needed it, Welly figured, as with fear-widened eyes, he watched great breakers bearing down upon them.

Earl watched these too, with keen appraisal. Edging the boat up toward the line of water where the crests broke, at the right second, he yelled, "Paddle like crazy!" Paddles flashed, and they shot over the next breaker while it was still rising, before it could tumble down in a foamy crash.

They were not long clear of the breakers when the wind hit. Where minutes before it had been only a salty breeze, it now hammered at them steadily, rising almost to a gale.

With Earl's special help, they moved on, but they were definitely slowed. The swells rising and falling under them became mountainous.

Welly's round face was as pale as his dusky skin allowed. To keep from screaming, he clamped his teeth and concentrated on the rhythmic swing of the paddles. Were warriors always this afraid, he wondered? Yet they do frightful things anyway. But then, so did he. Was that bravery? The thought made him grin—briefly.

Only by looking away from their goal occasionally could they tell they were moving closer to the jagged, wave-splashed rocks. They saw these now from a different angle than on the beach. Heather was intrigued by their bizarre shapes and watched them steadily. "Hey," she called, her words whipped back by the wind. "Look at that fantastic rock on the left. It has a hole in it!"

The other noticed it, too. Among the sky-thrusting fingers of rock rose one with a large irregular hole through it, worn by ages of swirling currents when it had lain just under the ocean's surface.

But now Earl's attention was drawn to something beyond the rocks. A thin gray fringe appeared along the horizon and slowly grew. He said nothing, but suggested everyone paddle harder.

In a few minutes Heather noticed it, too. "What's that out there, Earl? Is there a storm coming?"

"Don't think so, it's too low. Just keep paddling."

They watched it silently as with aching muscles they rhythmically dug into the dark water.

Finally Welly said, "It's a big wave, isn't it? A whole line of water."

Heather's throat went dry. "It's an illusion, like the last one."

"Afraid not," Earl answered grimly. "She's been busy out there making a real tidal wave this time. Morgan may lack imagination, but she's good at dealing with elements."

"Great," Welly muttered and paddled until he thought his arms would break off and sink.

The grayness was closer now and could clearly be seen as a gigantic wave. Earl redoubled his efforts physically and magically, but it didn't seem possible that they could reach the rocks in time or even that, once reached, they would prove any refuge.

The wind roared as the wave rolled steadily toward them. With scarcely a flinch, it passed over the rocks and continued bearing down on the fragile boat: A dark, towering wall of water, its top crested into a fringe of foam. In seeming slow motion the wave broke and began falling down upon them.

Heather and Welly stared upward, voiceless with horror. Earl lunged forward, grabbing their shoulders, and yelled, "Hold on to your paddles! Don't let loose of your paddles, no matter what!"

It seemed ludicrous advice, but they gripped their paddles furiously as the falling water hammered into them, driving them down toward the ocean bottom.

Heather felt the boat dissolve around her. She was tossed over and over with no discernible up or down. The air squeezed from her lungs, and her ears hummed. Then there was a movement she vaguely recognized as rising, and after endless moments, her head burst through the surface. Gasping wildly, she swallowed lungfuls of water and air. She coughed. Her head slipped beneath the waves, and again she was sinking.

Earl was shouting at her, shouting in her mind. "Your paddle! It's wood, old, dry wood! Grip it, concentrate on it, float like it, become like it. You are the wood. Light and buoyant, bobbing on the surface. Up and down over the waves."

Welly too heard and responded to Earl's hypnotic words, but almost sank again when, remembering his glasses, he grabbed at his face to hold them in place. It took long spluttering seconds to rebuild the illusion. The new mental image produced a stick of driftwood with an armlike branch that crooked up at one end.

Heather, now buoyant as her paddle, sped along on the surface, and her own mind freely supplied another image. She was like a storm-tossed ship, its carved figurehead bravely bearing down on the rocks.

And they were racing toward the cliffs! Already the long beach they had left so recently was sliding by far beneath them. She could almost feel the tearing hardness of the rocks beyond, as she hurtled toward them. They would be smashed!

A grip tightened painfully on her shoulder, moments before a jarring shock. Then blackness.

Welly opened his eyes, a surprising act, considering he was dead. He tried to focus on the cloud-smeared sky above him. He thought about limbs and muscles and tried to twitch a set that would theoretically move an arm. An arm did move in tingles of pain. No, it was asking too much to be dead, to be peacefully, painlessly dead.

He turned his head toward a groaning sound. Beside him, Earl lay face down in the sand. Feebly the older boy moved a hand. Then slowly he sat up, spitting out sand and coughing.

"Sorry," he gasped after a moment. "I tried to make that landing a little easier."

"May I let go now?" a thin voice quavered above them.

The two boys looked up and saw Heather clinging to her stick of driftwood, which was wedged firmly between two rocks. Earl staggered to his feet and caught her as she dropped. Together they toppled again onto the sand and narrowly escaped falling over a ledge.

Only then did they see where they were: a sand-filled crevass high on the cliffs that had once marked the ancient coast. Heather shivered and with still-numbed arms pulled herself back from the edge.

Already the incredible wave had slunk back into the sea. The gray depths churned with the huge undertow, while winds beat the surface into froth.

They'd lost their packs and coats in the water, and now, soaked and shivering, they huddled together on the wind-battered cliff, watching the tortured seascape below.

"I conclude," Welly said through chattering teeth, "that that wave was not illusion."

Earl groaned and shook some sand out of his hair. "No. She's good. That was some wave."

"Well, she's bent on finishing off your rocks now," Heather observed.

They looked out toward the rocks, which not long before had been their goal. From all sides waves tore into them, battering them mercilessly, tearing away huge chunks.

"She's certainly seeing to it there won't even be anything left to find there," Heather said heavily. "There won't even be any 'there' in a few minutes."

Earl stared glumly at the scene, but did not reply. He seemed to huddle into himself, his head sunk dejectedly on his knees. The sun dropped into a thick bank of cloud, spreading a sullen glow over the western sky. Against that backdrop, the jagged pillars and freak window of rock stood sharply silhouetted.

Behind the battered rock, the cloud curtain tore briefly, and the sun glowed redly through. Its bloody rays shot directly at them through the rocky portal.

Suddenly Heather stood up and looked quickly behind them. "Earl!" she cried. "Look! Look at the light!"

He raised his head and followed her gaze. "Of course!" he exclaimed. "I should have guessed! That rock wasn't our goal at all. Only a signpost—pointing here!"

Even as he spoke, a mighty wave crashed against the pierced rock and toppled it into the sea. Behind it, the sun sank below the watery horizon, but not before its beams had shown them the dark cleft between two tumbled stones, stones still entwined with faintly carved vines.

"Quickly!" Earl yelled. "Before she sees or guesses!"

Grabbing them by their shoulders, he propelled them toward the dark opening. Heather slipped quickly through, but Welly balked at the narrow gap.

"No time for qualms," Earl said, shoving him into the opening.

Three feet into the darkness, Welly stuck fast, wedged between grating rocks. A wave of panic hit him worse than in the old Welsh mine. He felt Earl apply a foot firmly to the small of his back, and suddenly he popped through.

Grabbing up his staff, Earl crowded after him as the wind outside rose to a vengeful shriek. Ahead, they faced darkness more total that any they'd ever imagined

✤ f i f t e e n ✤

LEGEND'S RETURN

"EARL." HEATHER'S VOICE SOUNDED SMALL AND BRITTLE IN the utter darkness. "Do you think you can give us a light?"

"I doubt it," he said close beside her. "In Avalon, my puny magic isn't worth a thing."

He stamped his staff sharply on the rock and muttered some words. "Nothing. Here, let's just hold hands and move carefully. We were allowed through the first gate, so there oughtn't to be any traps."

Tucking his staff under an arm, he fumbled for their hands, and slowly they shuffled through the blackness. On either side, Heather and Welly felt rough rock walls slip by beneath their fingers. The stone floor was uneven, but took no sudden drops.

The walls were becoming damp. Their fingers recoiled at the first touch of spongy moss. Glowing with a faint violet phosphorescence, these patches seemed to swim in the darkness before them. As the moss became denser, the light faintly showed the way and cast an eerie radiance over their faces.

The walls and floors glistened with damp, and here and there they heard the hollow drip of water over stone. They moved more confidently in the pale violet glow, but the farther they went, the less it felt as if they were traveling in a straight line. The sensation was of curling around themselves in ever-decreasing circles—like being trapped in a giant snail shell.

Ahead of them, they heard a faint musical chiming. As they drew closer, it seemed almost to have words interwoven, words they could never quite catch. It drew them on until, turning a corner, their eyes were assailed with light. They blinked in the brilliance. A patch of green-gold shone through a curtain of falling water. The drops, sparkling in the pure sunlight, cascaded over a rocky ledge. With silvery tinkling they fell into a clear pool edged about with moss and ferns.

The three pulled up at the beauty of the scene. Earl sighed deeply, like a traveler coming home. "Well, no stopping now," he said after a long moment. Tightly gripping their hands, he pulled them after him through the pool and the veil of sparkling drops.

The water was tingling cold, but before they could gasp they were through and standing on thick green grass. All about them the air was soft and warm, filled with a hazy golden light. Everything was of such aching loveliness, it brought tears to their eyes.

On all sides grew trees such as Heather and Welly had seen only in pictures, great stately trunks with graceful branches that spread into a canopy overhead. Leaves fluttering in the breeze filtered the sunlight in shifting patterns of gold and green. The grass underfoot was thick and soft and scattered over with tiny white flowers. From trees and bushes and the clear blue sky came mingled birdsong.

Earl smiled, but could find no words. None of them

could. He began walking through the arched trees, and the others followed, bemused with wonder.

On every side some new loveliness lay casually about, as though natural and not indescribably precious. Undisturbed by their passage, animals rested or fed in sun-drenched glades, animals they'd seen in books or scarcely imagined in dreams. With barely audible whirrings, rainbow-winged insects flitted through the air.

The grass sloped down to a shallow pond, its edge fringed in wind-ruffled reeds. Earl peeled off this travel-worn jacket and flopped down on the grass. Breathing its sweetness, he lay back and looked into the depths of blue sky. The others joined him. There was a gauzy timelessness in the air, as though a single moment had been snatched from some eternal dream.

Sitting up, at last, Earl removed his wet boots and socks and dug his toes into the cool grass. Laughing, he jumped up and waded out into the pool, rippling its clear green water.

"Come on!" he yelled to his two friends.

"Are you sure it's all right?" Heather asked. It was so beautiful here that, happy as it made her, she felt somehow out of place.

"Of course it's all right! The water does wonders for sore feet."

Boots and socks quickly discarded, the two joined him. The smooth coolness of the water lapped about their ankles, soaking into travel-weary feet like a healing balm.

Earl waded out farther and then to the others' surprise let out a joyous yell and dove into the water. For seconds the glassy surface closed over him, then he burst through it in a shower of emerald drops. Laughing, he splashed glittering arches of water toward them. They splashed back.

At last, ending the water war, Earl sat down chest deep in the pond and splashed his arms in great angel wings, watching the cascading drops sparkle in the sun.

"Boys will always be boys, I see," said a soft, musical voice behind them.

Earl spluttered to a stop and stood up in the water, looking embarrassed. Water dripped from his dark hair over his face. "Lady," he said sheepishly.

The woman laughed. "It's a good deal younger you are, then when we last saw you, Merlin. But you are unmistake-able and always welcome, as are any you bring."

Heather and Welly turned to see a woman more lovely than imagining. Her gown was of sun light sparkling upon water, and her hair an aurora of light caught with shifting rainbows. The delicacy of her face seemed carved from a precious gem, but it was softer and glowed with a golden warmth.

She smiled, her blue eyes bright with laughter, and she held out her hands to Earl as he waded from the pool, dripping water and looking abashed.

"Lady," he said with a bow, "these are my friends and companions, Wellington Jones and Heather McKenna; without them I would probably not be here."

Smiling, she took them both by the hand. "You are welcome indeed. It is good to know that Merlin has found himself such stout friends. We knew he had awakened, but didn't know how he might fare in that world of yours, nor when he would seek one of the few doors left open." She looked at them, a smile playing softly on her lips. "I expect you will all have tales worth telling, and as your friend can tell you, we are very fond of tales here."

Heather and Welly smiled up at her, but could find no words that seemed fine enough. Earl, however, said, "Lady, where is—?"

"Merlin! Two thousand years, and you are still as impatient as ever. One would think your mixed blood might mellow you some. But then, I suppose wizards are a law unto themselves."

Earl hung his head in chagrin, but the lady laughed and

placed a hand on his shoulder. "We wouldn't want you to change, friend; you are needed as you are. Yes, I'll take you to him soon. But first, I think these children can use some rest and refreshment. And as you seem to be a growing boy again, you also might want a taste of the food Avalon offers its guests."

Welly was delighted at the prospect of food, but Heather said, "Oh, Lady, just being here is enough. It's all so lovely!" She stopped, surprised at her own temerity, but the lady only smiled sadly.

"I am glad it pleases you, child. But it hurts to hear how lovely you find it. Once our two worlds were very close, as close as a mirror and that which it reflects. They grew apart, but even as Merlin first knew them, one could still see the original in the reflection. Now, I'm afraid your world is a pale reflection indeed, and it saddens us."

As she talked, she led them away from the pond to a small sun-filled meadow where other beings as lovely as herself awaited them. Some seemed human or partly so, while others were definitely something else. Several greeted Earl like old friends and led the three to seats of sun-warmed rocks. There they were brought food and drink in crystal plates and goblets.

The food was lovely to the eyes and every bite or sip had its own unique flavor, too fine and rare ever to be repeated. In the air around them was music of wind and pipes and laughter. They relaxed on the grass under the vast blue sky. Golden afternoon slipped into dusky twilight and then into glorious night. The sky glittered with a myriad of stars.

They woke the next morning, or perhaps many mornings after, stretched comfortably on the grass. The lady was with them and offered to lead them to Arthur.

"He was sorely wounded when he came to us," she told Earl as they left the meadow. "But gradually we healed him, his body at least, and returned him to his youth and vigor. His other wounds . . . they were healed perhaps by time. We didn't wish him to forget, only to rest and wait."

They had come to the shore of a large lake, gleaming like a golden mirror in the sun. The lady led them into a shallow leaf-shaped boat. Of its own power, it moved out over the water, gliding silently past white swans, who turned their necks to watch them pass. Heather trailed her fingers through the smooth water, then lifted them to watch the falling drops catch the light. They slid onto the fine white sand of the other shore. There the lady led them to the base of a high hill, steep and rocky. As they climbed, a stiff breeze played about their hair and over the grass.

At the crest, the air was perfumed by a grove of flowering trees, their silver-gray trunks gnarled with age. Fallen blossoms floated along the surface of a brook, which they followed to its source, a spring bubbling up in a quiet glade. Low in the grass was a moss-softened rock, and on it lay a man sleeping.

He was a young man, scarcely more than a boy. His skin was pale and clear. A shock of golden hair fell over a rough-carved face, softened by sleep and by youth. He seemed deeply asleep, as though floating in distant peaceful dreams.

For a moment Earl stood looking down at him. Then with a sob he sank to his knees. Reaching for the young man's hand, he dropped his forehead upon it.

After a time, the man stirred and opened his eyes. Blue and blurry at first, they focused on the lady. "Ah, Lady, you have such long dreams here." He sighed. ". . . and such rest."

The dark head raised beside him, and the man stared into the gaunt tear-streaked face.

"But who . . . ?" He looked more closely. "Merlin, is it you?"

"One who scarcely hoped to see you living again, my Lord."

Arthur laughed and sat up. "I can't say how I knew you,

old wizard! Aren't you just a trifle younger than when I saw you last?"

His friend smiled. "Don't rub it in, youngster! Last I saw you, you were a hardened, battle-scarred warrior with streaks of gray in your golden beard."

The two laughed and hugged each other as friends might after several millennia.

Time had little reality there, but in its own way it passed and was spent renewing old acquaintances and forging new ones. Arthur and several of the denizens of Avalon listened with concern as Earl, Heather and Welly related the events of their own recent lives.

Arthur's concern deepened as they reconstructed the happenings in their world since he and Merlin had left it. In the end, it was a picture of heartbreaking sadness: great struggle, beauty and achievement overlain with a wash of hate, stupidity and inexcusable waste. Afterwards, it seemed that not even the beauty and peace of Avalon could raise Arthur's spirits.

But to Heather and Welly, although their own world was harsh, it was something to be accepted not mourned over. And Avalon was a life apart, a sweetness to be savored. They spent the golden days and crystal nights wandering through its beauties or in companionship with its inhabitants. Waterfolk taught them swimming, and after initial trepidation on Welly's part, it seemed as natural as it would to a fish.

But Earl spent his time with Arthur, and the two wandered restlessly over the Eldritch lands.

The mists of another morning were rising as they walked the rim of a high waterfall. Blue, rainbowed clouds rose from the chasm where the slender column of water crashed among the rocks. Moss-hung cypress sighed and whispered among themselves, and the breeze was scented with sage and wild thyme.

Arthur kicked a loose pebble over the edge and waited to hear it clatter and bounce on the rocks far below. "What I don't understand, Merlin, is why they didn't tell me. I wasn't sleeping all that time. And they knew what was happening out there. True, some of them lost interest, things have strayed so far apart. But the lady and others, they watch, they know! Why didn't they tell me what was happening, how our dreams were faring—what succeeded and what failed, and how the whole thing drove itself insanely off a cliff? It was my world. They should have told me!"

"Arthur, what good would that cruelty have done? You, a mortal, were brought here close to death. Their desire was to see you healed, to have you rest as you deserved, and to wait."

"Yes, wait. But for what? Merlin, by some alchemy I'll never understand, you were locked away waiting to be freed. Then as soon as you were, or remembered that you were, you came looking for me. So, this time of waiting is over. But why? What good can I do? One former king, in a world infinitely more wrong than any we knew."

"That world needs you, Arthur."

"Needs me! That's what you said before. But I was young then, truly young. It was exciting, exhilarating. I was to be king! But, Merlin, I know what that all means now. I've gone through it once. Certainly there was pride and beauty and satisfaction, but there was also pain, failure and loss. Being kin isn't being revered and leading troops to glory. It's taking on other people's pains and problems, being responsible for their lives and happiness and sacrificing your own. Merlin, I loved and was betrayed! I built and saw what I built destroyed! Are you asking me to go through all that again?"

"Arthur, do you really want me to answer that?"

"Yes! I mean, no. Oh, you infuriating old man! You're going to lecture me. I know exactly what you're going to say. And I don't want to hear it!" He yanked a fern out of the dark soil and tore it to shreds.

His companion sat down on a stone and turned his attention to the splendid view across the gorge.

After several minutes, Arthur threw the remains of the fern over the edge. "Your problem, Merlin, is that you haven't the decency to be wrong now and again."

"Oh, I've had my moments."

"But this isn't one of them, is it?" Arthur dropped heavily onto a mossy bank. "You and the folk of Avalon say I'm needed there. I don't understand that now any more than I did before. If it's true, it also seems I can't avoid it any more than before. But you can't blame me for wanting to! This time, after all, I know what I'm in for."

The people of Avalon prepared the four mortals for their departure. New warm clothes were made and spread in readiness under the trees. The hooded fur cloaks seemed alien in this world of perpetual summer.

Earl set about giving Arthur a crash course in the culture of the strange new world he was entering. On the question of language, however, the teacher despaired, and at last complained to the lady.

"Arthur can talk easily with everyone here and can't seem to grasp that Avalon has its own laws but that out there the language has changed. If he tried to converse in his native tongue, he'd be unintelligible. And, Lady, I know from experience that Arthur's a dunce with languages. He's a fine leader, a great warrior and many other things. But if I try to teach him a new language, we'll be here another two thousand years!"

She laughed. "It's not that we don't love our guests, but it looks as if I'd better make him a gift of the language and spare you the tutoring."

"Bless you, Lady. For me that gift is beyond price!"

There were other gifts as well. Arthur's mighty sword

was reforged and returned to him. But although offered more elegant alternatives, Earl preferred his small hawk-headed sword and the pine staff from the banks of the Tamar. This last, he said, was tied to the world in which it must function.

Welly and Heather also chose to keep their swords from the ancient Eldritch wreck. But new sheaths were made for them of soft pale leather worked with designs of twining vines and interlocking spirals.

At last came the eve of their departure. The four travelers sat in the meadow where the three had passed their first night. The lady was with them, along with others of their friends. In the center of the meadow a fire blazed, not for warmth and light, but as a symbol of fellowship and belonging that spanned time and worlds.

The lady looked across the fireglow at the four and saw that all followed their own thoughts. But the young boy and girl seemed particularly troubled.

"Heather, there is something you want, isn't there?"

"Yes, there is." She stopped twisting her braid and looked up. "There were many things I wanted that don't seem important now. And what I wanted most, I never realized—just to be needed."

The other smiled with understanding. "But, Lady," Heather continued, "Avalon is so beautiful. I'm afraid, when we go, we'll forget it, like some dream. Our world is different. It is mine and I can accept it, but to carry a small candle of memory would make it easier."

The lady nodded. "The contrast will be painful. It might be best for you if it did fade. But yes, you may keep it. Like a good dream, let it stay in the back of your mind, to be called on when needed."

She looked at Welly. "And this will be for you as well. But do I sense you need something more?"

He blushed and stared down at his hands. "Well, I guess I understand things better, too. I know what I can do, and maybe something of what should be done. But . . . oh, it's nothing grand. It's stupid and selfish . . . but I still wish I had good eyes and didn't need glasses."

She placed a soft hand on his. "I suppose some sorts of magic could do that, but it's really not our way. We don't wish to a make a person other than he is or change what he has made of himself. We can heal a wound or sickness. But, Welly, your eyes are neither. They are part of what makes you. Can you understand that at all?"

Welly smiled weakly. "I guess so."

She put her hands on his shoulders and looked him in the face. "But you needn't be downcast." She laughed. "Perhaps there are a few things we can do. For one thing, I suspect the prescription could be improved. And perhaps a charm to keep you from breaking or losing the things?"

He nodded and saw with surprise that the circles of glass before his eyes were clearer than before, focusing everything in sharp detail. And they rested on his head with a strange new security. He looked up with a confident smile.

Talk in the meadow merged with sleep, ending in the radiance of Avalon's predawn glow. After a final meal, the four, wearing their new warm clothing, hoisted fresh packs on their backs. The lady alone led them up a pine-clad hill. The ground was carpeted with needles and the air scented with their spice.

Near the crest of the hill, the lady halted and kissed each lightly on the forehead. They took one last look at her and the beautiful land behind. Then, Arthur in the lead, they stepped between two tall pines into utter darkness. The scent of warm pine lingered for a moment, then was gone.

This time Welly and Heather walked confidently through the blackness. Their steps echoed as from high-vaulted walls, and cold began seeping out of the stone around them. At last a patch of gray appeared ahead. They stepped out of an ancient tomb, snow resting quietly in the spirals carved into its fallen stones.

The light was cold, and the sky a blank gray. Below them, a new landscape stretched bleak and treeless. Wind whipped over the snow, hurling dry, icy flakes into their faces.

The contrast with what they had left was stark, but to Welly and Heather the air carried a tang of home.

After a long silence, Arthur turned to Earl. "Do you know where we are?" he asked tautly.

"Someplace in Britain. But the lady didn't say exactly where this gate would lead."

"And the time of year?"

"Time passes differently in the two worlds. But from what she said, I'd guess April."

"April," Arthur repeated. "April in Britain! How can this have happened? There should be trees budding; there should be daffodils and new green grass. We should hear cuckoos in the woods and see larks soaring in the sky—a clear blue sky!"

His face was pained as he looked at his friend. "Merlin, can we really do anything? Is there anything here worth fighting for?"

"There are people left here. People and the glimmer of hope they hold."

He was silent for a moment, then continued. "Arthur, you said you'd been through it before. You didn't relish coming back, because you knew what you were in for. But maybe, because we do know what we're in for, we can do better this time. We know our mistakes and the ones made after us. Maybe we can see the danger signals. Maybe we can set things on the right road so this doesn't happen again."

Arthur smiled grimly. "Maybe so. But it's rather an uphill road."

"Yes, it is," Merlin replied. Then his dark eyes flashed with a smile, and he spread his arms exultantly. "But look what you have to start with! A wise old adolescent wizard, and two seasoned young campaigners, dropouts from the best school in Wales! What quest ever began in better company?"

Young Arthur Pendragon threw back his head and laughed. The sound rang like a bell over the silent landscape. "Now that's a quest I want to be a part of! Let's be on our way!"

Four cloaked figures walked down the hillside as the snow about them turned a soft, fragile pink. In the eastern sky, the veiled sun rose on a new day.

about the author

Growing up in California, Pamela F. Service developed interests in politics, history and science fiction. She received a bachelor's degree from the University of California and a master's degree from the University of London. She has pursued her interest in history by touring ancient sites and digging in excavations in Britain and the Sudan.

Ms. Service currently lives in Bloomington, Indiana, with her husband and daughter. She is the curator of a local museum, is active in politics and is at work on her next young adult novel.

Have you met the PRATT SISTERS

?

...Young Adult Novels by

CYNTHIA BLAIR